Taming the Beast

DISCIPLINING
THE BEAST

TINA DONAHUE

Disciplining the Beast
ISBN # 978-1-83943-826-4
©Copyright Tina Donahue 2018
Cover Art by Emmy @studioenp ©Copyright November 2018
Interior text design by Claire Siemaszkiewicz
Totally Bound Publishing

DISCIPLINING
THE BEAST

Dedication

To Pamela Leonhardt, my awesome PA and to
my street team — Tina's Romance Rebels.
Ladies, I couldn't have done this without you.

Chapter One

Wynona lifted her face and sniffed.

A vulnerable soul. Its fragrance was a mixture that combined fragile life, everlasting death, sweet innocence and decadent sin — each an aphrodisiac to a reaper.

She gripped her desk to stay put rather than snatching the lovely spirit. She'd been a bad girl in the past, stealing souls without authorization, and was paying big time for that now. The powers that be had banished her to this godforsaken place — From Crud to Stud, a New Orleans makeover service for supernatural beings.

Weres howled, vamps hissed, zombies moaned.

The scent beckoned once more, tempting her beyond restraint. She gritted her teeth and tried to focus on her stupid paperwork. Her concentration and resolve wavered. Maybe if she simply looked at the potential victim but didn't touch, everything would be all right.

She stalked down the hall.

A female staff member ground to a quick halt, pivoted and hurried into a treatment room. Other doors closed before Wynona could pass, telling her what she'd already known. No one liked reapers, not even otherworldly beings who didn't have souls to lose. Given that she couldn't hurt them as she would a mortal, they could have at least tried to be cordial and said "Hi" or shot the breeze. Made her feel like a team member rather than a pariah.

Another door closed. More than a few staffers inside threw the locks.

Ignoring their snubs, she focused on Heather, the receptionist. Her blindingly white dress matched her pale hair and skin. As a good fairy, she healed those in pain and radiated kindness needed by the lonely. Her soul was pure as a baby's first breath and off-limits.

Rather than look at her computer, Heather smiled sweetly at someone Wynona couldn't see.

She drew closer. At her approach, the lights flickered from the vibes she gave off. She likened it to an early warning system that let mortals and supernaturals know she was in the area and they had better watch out. As if she didn't already have enough problems snatching souls. This she didn't need.

Heather lifted her face to the pulsing lights then looked at the hall.

Wynona arched one eyebrow in greeting.

Rather than offer a nod, grin or a "Hey, how you doing?" in return, Heather's lovely face grew even ashier. She fumbled in her desk drawer, yanked out a crucifix and held it up like actors did in those old Dracula movies. Her hands shook. "I'm sorry. This is rude, I know, but— I'm sorry."

Wynona wasn't certain whether to laugh at Heather's apologetic nature, groan at being treated so lousily or surrender to the status quo and skulk back to her office to hide out until someone needed her. The soul fragrance swirled near, pulling her closer. "No offense taken."

"Please stay where you are."

She couldn't and picked up speed.

Constance rounded the corner.

Wynona reared back.

So did Constance. Her silky gown swished around her ample curves, the hot-pink color complementing her ebony complexion. She took in Wynona then Heather.

"Put that down." Constance jabbed her thumb at the cross. "That's for vamps, not reapers, unless you want to whack her on the head to get her to back off."

Wynona lifted her chin. "From doing what? I was merely walking down the hall."

"Uh-huh." Constance gave her a knowing look. "Say the word and I can make you forget everything you were about to do."

Big talk. However, Constance was a damn good voodoo priestess with a talent for removing memories. Once her bejeweled fingers touched anyone's skull, poof, the past was history. "How about you touch me and I touch you in return?"

"Wynona." Heather's cheeks pinked up. "You shouldn't talk like that."

Strange advice from a good fairy who has a thing going with a lusty former satyr and counts a nympho genie as her BFF. "I wasn't taking about sex, hon."

Heather went into a full-body blush.

Constance huffed. "No reaping here, got it? Especially staff members' souls."

"Yes, ma'am. But how about ones from clients who are still alive?" She itched to get past her to the source emitting the delicious fragrance. From where she stood, she still couldn't see everything in the reception area.

Feathery ferns and potted plants overran the cozy space, making it a veritable forest. Faux gas fixtures graced the coral walls. Coming in here was like stepping back in time, the dated, romantic feel a cover for what really went on. Moonlight therapy for weres. Treatments to tame bloodsucking vamps. Speech and personality programs for zombies. Potions for every purpose so supernatural beings could move among the unsuspecting and get it on with mortal babes.

Constance squared her shoulders. "We don't bite the hands that feed us. Behave yourself and get back to work."

"Wait." Heather stood. "There's someone here to see you, Wynona."

Hmm. No one ever willingly approached her except another reaper who had nothing to lose. Just once, she'd like to browbeat a shifter into a treatment room and take out her frustration on him rather than her own kind. "Who wants to see me? Or rather, what?"

Heather bit her lower lip.

A sure sign another reaper awaited. Possibly one she'd dated only to have him dump her so he could tame his beast here and give a mortal woman his best. Just what she didn't need, another louse. She drooped.

Unfortunately, her disappointment didn't change things. She'd been put here as an enforcer to get the clients where they should be and strap them in or subdue them so other staff members could work their magic. If a vamp, zombie or reaper got out of line or too frisky during treatment, it was her sworn duty to make them behave. If she didn't, there would be hell to pay. Literally. She passed Constance but didn't get far. Her legs refused to work.

The guy on the sofa pushed to his feet.

His scent washed over her, snatching her breath. If goodness and starshine had an odor, that would be his, the fragrance of an unsullied soul. Definitely not a reaper. Not a mortal, either.

That reality should have had her bolting down the hall before she did something bad.

His outstanding looks kept her rooted to the spot. He was a large man, six-three or more, with shoulders that went from here to tomorrow. His broad chest, flat belly and powerful thighs were the stuff of Greek myths wrapped in fashionable duds straight from *GQ* — charcoal-colored pants and a midnight-blue shirt. Both garments draped his form beautifully, including the impressive bulge behind his fly.

Apollo had nothing on this dude.

As far as she could tell, he was hung better than most gods and mortals. In human years, he was likely early to mid-thirties. He'd tied back his long raven hair, though a few silky strands had escaped to graze his forehead and firm jaw.

Her knees went watery.

Dark stubble dusted his cheeks, chin and upper lip. His complexion was a healthy bronze, eyes lushly lashed, their color a deeper blue than sapphires, his gaze deliciously intense.

Give him cuffs and a whip along with free rein and he'd rock a BDSM chamber any day.

Her insides went gooey.

Of course, the goodness rolling off him was a problem. He couldn't be here for a makeover. There was nowhere to go from perfect, unless...

He might want to release his beast, the same as Eric had done a few years back. As a direct descendant of Cupid, Eric had wanted to ditch his courtly demeanor and become a bad boy to snag the babes. After he'd met Becca, the half-witch who owned this joint, he'd changed his mind about other women and hooked up with her for life.

A sweet dream Wynona coveted but didn't expect for herself. However, if this guy wanted someone to corrupt him and had heard about her hardcore ways, how could she say no?

She sashayed across the room and stopped close enough for them to kiss. He didn't back up or take off. She liked that. Gave her a chance to indulge.

His full mouth had probably fueled countless female wet dreams, the cleft in his chin was beyond lickable and the interest in his gaze was the best of all. He searched her eyes the way a mortal did when wanting to touch another person's soul.

If she'd had one, she wouldn't have let him look inside. Being defenseless led to more sorrow and hurt. *No, thank you.* She'd had an eternity dealing with that crap. "Hey there, I'm Wynona."

She would have offered to shake his hand, but one touch from a reaper and anyone alive was toast, except for select supernatural beings. As a rule, those whose powers were equal to or greater than hers. She wanted to ask him what he was but waited, hoping skin-to-skin contact wouldn't be verboten for them.

"Wynona." He inclined his head. A lock fell past his ear and skimmed his cheek.

Her mouth watered.

"I'm Rafael."

Indeed, he was. A killer name for a sexy man. "And what brings you here tonight, Rafael?"

"You."

He couldn't have given a better answer. Her spirits soared. "So, you've heard of me, huh?"

"Repeatedly and at length." His cheeks darkened.

She flushed with excitement too. "What kind of makeover did you want?"

"I don't. That is, none." He glanced past her to Heather and Constance.

Heather pretended to work rather than eavesdrop. Constance didn't budge, all eyes and ears. Stefin, a demon enforcer, had joined her.

He and the other male enforcement team had given Wynona a fucking hard time from the second she'd started at this place. She glared at him.

He glowered right back, the flames in his eyes blazing.

She spoke to Rafael. "None? You mean, as in, no taming your beast? So, you're here to free your wayward urges, right?"

His forehead turned red but desire flashed in his eyes. "No. I need to rein yours in."

Her hope spiked a thousand percent. "You're into BDSM too?" She smiled slyly. "You like being a Master?"

Heather made a strangled noise.

Constance offered a throaty moan that sounded beyond turned on.

Rafael had stopped breathing seconds ago. He pulled in some air. "I'm your parole officer."

Wynona went colder than a vamp then hotter than a menopausal woman. "What? Wait. I know what my parole officer looks like. Little dude with a face only a blind mother could love and a personality on par with overcooked spaghetti." Her gesture took in Rafael's magnificence. "Definitely not you."

"Hold it." Stefin strode to them, his long blond hair bobbing with each step. "She was in prison, like me?"

During his mortal days, he'd been in the Russian mafia, which had landed him a front seat in Hell.

Rafael wrinkled his nose. Heather sprayed her baby powder scent. The fragrance did little to eliminate the sulfur stench exuded by Stefin and all demons.

Rafael backed away from him. "We're trying to avoid prison for Wynona. The group sent me here to make certain she behaves."

Stefin nodded. "What group is that?"

"Supernatural Authority in Charge of Souls, what else?" Wynona curled her upper lip at him. "SACS for short. They suck, just like you do." She faced Rafael. "What happened to the other guy?"

"Got kicked upstairs."

"Because he made my existence miserable?"

Stefin wedged himself between her and Rafael. "Tell me how to get rid of her...Wynona." He made a gagging sound from speaking her name for once. "I'll do it for free. I could even pay you for the information. We have leather restraints here, manacles for the problem cases — rope, too. Whatever we need. There are countless storage facilities around. We can tie her up and dump her in one of them. As long as we pay the fee, no one will ever know she's there."

Constance cleared her throat. "Wynona would."

Stefin waved dismissively.

Heather tried to frown, not an easy thing for a good fairy. "No one should hurt her or anyone else. Maybe you guys should talk in her office where it's private."

"Good idea." Stefin pivoted and gestured to lead the way.

Constance grabbed his arm. "Not you, Wynona and Rafael. Go on." She flicked her hand at them. "We'll give you guys all the time you need."

Now, she wants to be friendly.

Wynona tramped down the hall, teeth bared. A were halted just outside a treatment room, spotted her and ducked back inside.

She would have followed and locked Rafael out if it would have done her any good.

Of all the rotten luck. She'd just gotten her last guy to back off and now she had a new one to break in or break. Whatever it took. Even if Rafael smelled better than a squeaky-clean soul and was hotter than a romance cover model, he was still the enemy.

She stopped at her office and gestured him inside.

He backed into the snug space, gaze boring into hers—a warning not to pull anything.

Commanding and hot. The whole enchilada.

She trembled in delight and hated herself for it.

After locking the door, she waved her hand at the lone chair in here. "Take it. I'm good." She sat on her desk, crossed her legs and leaned forward, giving him an eyeful. Her skintight top plumped her breasts. Unlike other reapers, who used fear to corner their prey, she employed seduction…snug leather outfits, along with her signature scent, a lavender and musk combo. When she hunted, the poor slobs didn't know what had hit them.

Rafael dropped into his seat. The springs creaked. "About you stealing souls."

There was that. She was supposed to wait for instructions from on high before swiping the things. Trouble was, when creeps crossed her path and hurt innocents or pissed her off, they weren't long for this earth. "I've made a few mistakes."

He looked heavenward and breathed deeply.

His prominent Adam's apple was kickass, the same as his rumbling voice. Each time he spoke, his baritone registered in her belly.

"We've heard of more than a few mishaps." He pulled a smartphone from his pants pocket and reading glasses from his shirt pocket.

The specs made him look even more intelligent and sexier than sin. She gripped the desk to avoid crawling on his lap. Later, maybe, when he'd loosened up some.

He scrolled down the phone's display. "Jerome James. Remember him?"

Did she ever. "Uh…"

"He was crossing the street in front of this place and dropped to the ground. Gone in a flash. He was twenty-three and in perfect health until that moment." Rafael peered over his glasses. "Any idea what happened?"

The flecks of green in his eyes took her breath away. "Uh…"

"I'll need more than that."

If he was looking for a confession, he was out of luck. An apology wasn't doable, either. She'd been justified in taking Jerome down. The day she'd checked him out, he'd been unbelievably rude, shoving past people and stomping on her toes. He'd knocked against an elderly woman who could barely totter, even though she used a walker. She should have cracked his skull with the thing, but she'd been too busy trying to stay on her swollen feet. He hadn't noticed or cared. Rather than using an iPod with earbuds for his crappy music, he'd carried a boombox, the bass turned thunderously loud. His soul had stunk from entitlement and cruelty, especially to women. He'd asked for it. "Can we bring him back?"

"Already have. Different body."

She hadn't expected that. "A woman's?"

Rafael frowned. "No, a male."

Too bad, since Jerome needed to see things from the other side. "How's he doing? What's his address and phone number? Maybe I should apologize."

Rafael arched one dark eyebrow.

What a luscious bastard. "If he's having trouble adjusting, I could help him out." Break his kneecaps, too, if he was still a jerk. "Anything for the team." She swung her foot.

He glanced at her leather boot, the tip close to his leg. If she moved a tad more, she'd be able to touch him.

Perspiration beaded on his forehead. He scooted back. "About what you did to Pete Tremore..."

Another guy who'd lacked manners. Newly turned vamps were the absolute worst. "Never heard of him."

Rafael's gaze roamed her thigh. "The report states you and he dated for several months."

Until he'd dumped her for a mortal. A guy, no less, who had season tickets to numerous sports events. What a jerk Pete had turned out to be. If she could have taken his soul, she would have. "I'm free now. Totally unencumbered and ready to roll."

Rafael stared hard.

If he thought that was going to intimidate her, he was dead wrong. She'd rarely been this turned on before and gave him a mischievous smile. "Is good cop gone? Are you going to be bad cop now? Mix things up?"

"This is why I waited for you in the reception area rather than coming here."

"To avoid having this conversation?"

"To see what would happen. When I arrived, I told Heather not to buzz you. I wanted to gauge how long you'd last before losing control. You got through five seconds." He pointed at her. "You wanted to take my soul out there, admit it."

Well, hell, she'd wanted to enjoy every part of him, especially his mouth and family jewels, until she'd learned who he was. A freaking good angel who was basically all soul and squeaky clean. Talk about lousy breaks. "Maybe I should call a lawyer and clam up until he or she gets here. Know any good ones?"

"Do you want to spend your entire existence in confinement? You may not like Hell."

"I hear the BDSM clubs are epic down there."

"Not for someone in solitary."

She pushed out her bottom lip. "Would you do that to me?"

He stared at her mouth, hair and boobs, lingering on each part for an indecently long time.

Her pussy creamed.

Someone or something rammed into the wall behind her. The framed business license tapped the plaster. Howls filled the hall. Voices bled into her office. "Don't, don't, don't!"

Stefin growled. "Exactly. *Don't* force me to put you back in that room."

"Get away from me."

"When you're through with your treatment."

"No."

Stefin cursed in his thick Russian accent.

Rafael focused on her legs and rack.

"Hey, what's going on here?" Zoe, the enforcement team manager, had just joined the fray. "Quit clawing the wall." Her voice was as gravelly as someone who'd guzzled acid. "I mean it."

An agonized shriek broke through the other racket, then everyone chilled. Footfalls and thumps followed.

Wynona figured Zoe had stomped on the uncooperative client's foot, distracting him enough so Stefin could throw him back into the treatment room.

Everything grew quiet. She uncrossed her legs.

Rafael lifted his face and met her eyes.

Time stopped. Her breathing did, too. Lust raced through her, coupled with too much longing. He was such a beautiful guy, his caution gone, replaced by... She wasn't entirely certain what the emotion was, but it looked like wonder. A balm for a lonely reaper who'd known countless rejections. Who everyone treated like a leper.

Not that he'd be any different in the long run. As he'd said, he was her parole officer. He'd make her behave, threatening her with solitary in Hell, rather than whips, crops, cuffs and chains, playing alpha to her sub, disciplining her inner beast the way she needed.

Once she was a good girl, he'd get kicked upstairs and someone else would come down to hassle her. Probably a troll like the last guy.

It wasn't fair. She needed to do her thing without interference. Being stuck here and feared or despised was bad enough. "Look, I know you're a busy man. Working for the Big Guy must be hell. To make things easier on you, I'll behave. Promise." She gave him the Boy Scout salute she'd learned from Pete. "I'll only take souls I should and even throw in a deep, wet, lingering kiss and a slap on the ass to send them on their way with a smile on their faces. How's that?"

His eyes had gone blurry when she'd mentioned *deep* and *wet*. He stared at her mouth. She moistened her lips. A scream rang from the next room. Numerous thumps punctuated the sound.

Rafael's shirt fluttered from his ragged breaths.

She battled to pull in any air.

He cleared his throat. "Every day."

"Sorry, what?"

He pocketed his smartphone and glasses. "I'm going to be here every day."

That could be a good thing or bad. Wary, she tried a submissive smile to give him an idea of what she'd like during their down time. "Why?"

"To keep you in line. Make certain you don't steal any more souls. We're running out of fresh bodies to put them into."

Not what she wanted to hear. "Hey, is that my fault? Tell your boss to create more. He's the man. He can do anything."

"He already has, putting me in charge of you. Whether you like it or not, I'm going to protect you from yourself."

"Oh, yeah?" She swung her foot one last time and grazed his thigh. "Who's going to protect you?"

Rafael stood.

The room dipped and swayed. He clutched the chair and tried to clear his head. Wasn't possible. Her flowery fragrance invaded his senses and called to mind women from way back when, whose smiles were gentle, gazes modest and their morals impeccable.

Wynona was light years from that.

Her black top, jeans and boots fit like skin, the leather molded to her slender yet curvy figure, her breasts ripe, hips lavish, legs long. No woman's mouth was plusher. Sensuality poured from her. In the harsh overhead light, her hair was whiter than fresh snow, the ends dangling to her waist. Her silvery eyes were unearthly, her alabaster complexion the only delicate thing about her.

She was the most gorgeous female he'd ever seen.

From reading her file, he knew she was a creature of passion and wasn't afraid to get her hands dirty — or any other part of her, for that matter. He couldn't imagine her in the missionary position during sex unless she was on top, driving a man crazy and corrupting his soul.

Good times.

He shook his head to clear it. The room lurched worse than before. With his face down, he staggered away.

Her spike heels tapped the floor. "You're not planning to go through my files, are you?"

He had one arm slung over the metal cabinet to steady himself. "Nope."

"Then what are you doing?"

Pulling myself together, if I'm lucky. "I need to make a report to my boss. Be right back."

He walked through the wall. An easy matter for an angel. Not so good for the people on the other side.

There were four beings in this treatment room. Given the sulfur smell and flickering flames in their eyes, they were demons. One was a short female with a nice figure, though nowhere near as epic as Wynona's.

He rubbed his forehead.

This woman had long black hair, an ivory complexion, rosy nipples and dark curls between her legs. Other than her high heels, she wore nothing except a surprised look and lifted her slender eyebrows at him.

Stefin was also nude, balls pulled tight to his groin, his cock hard as stone and pointing at the female demon's pussy. "Rafael, hey. Stefin here."

The black demon shook his head. His dreadlocks danced over his shoulders.

The redheaded demon eyed Stefin with dismay and sighed loudly. "Cretin."

"Sorry." Rafael backed up. "Didn't mean to intrude."

"I'm the cretin." Stefin slammed his fist into his chest. "Not you." He growled at the redheaded demon with the country-western accent. "At least I know how to charm a woman, especially my Zoe." He wrapped his arm around the female, presumably his Zoe. "What's your excuse besides being a hick?"

"Least I got some brains."

"Yeah, where the sun don't shine."

"Hold it." Zoe put out her hands. She glared at Rafael. Smoke puffed from her hair. "Do. You. Mind? We're on break. We only have fifteen minutes, two of which were already wasted on a stubborn were."

The black demon patted her ass. "Relax, *chérie*." He had a lilting French accent. "What we don't finish now, we can save for our dinner break."

The other guys snuggled close.

She moaned. They grunted.

Rafael walked through the next wall. A woman in a white uniform lay on a treatment table, a vampire huddled over her, his mouth on her neck.

She glanced at Rafael. Her lust-slitted lids snapped open. She shoved the vamp away.

He windmilled his arms to right himself and staggered this way and that, at last slumping against the wall. "Hey, babe, what's the deal?"

She pointed at Rafael.

The vamp looked over. Saliva dripped from his fangs.

After shooting to a sitting position, she zipped her uniform to cover her lacy white bra. "This isn't what it looks like. See, no marks." She pointed at her neck.

The hickey there was nearly as large as Rafael's fist, the center bright red, the edges purple.

The vamp leaned in. "She means no puncture wounds." He puffed up. "I didn't drink one drop of her damned blood, even though I wanted to."

She beamed. "He's been such a good boy."

"Saving all my moves for later, in bed." He winked.

Holding back a groan, Rafael unfurled his retractable wings and rose through the ceiling. He was willing to risk running into drones or birds to get away from too much temptation.

What kind of operation does Becca Salt run? The paperwork said she owned a makeover service, not a brothel with staff and clients who were equally depraved. Sending Wynona to this halfway house had been a mistake, but there hadn't been anywhere else to put her besides here or the lowest levels in Hell. Places even Satan wouldn't visit.

From Crud to Stud had seemed the perfect solution. No one there was fully mortal, so taking their souls wasn't an option for her. She could scare them, sure, especially sweet Heather, but couldn't go further than that.

Of course, the neighborhood outside the service teemed with mortals, their lives and souls ready for harvest by her, an RR or rebel reaper.

Pickings were good tonight.

The mild weather had brought out tourists and locals gearing up for Halloween. Plastic skulls, glowing jack-o-lanterns and fake spider webs decorated storefronts. A bluesy tune poured from a bar. People shouted and laughed. Horns honked. Horse-drawn carriages clattered down the street. A soft breeze carried numerous scents — booze, seared meat, spicy Cajun fare.

None drove away Wynona's fragrance, sweet yet musky, reserved but seductive.

Rafael shivered in pleasure when he shouldn't have. He had business to conduct and forced himself to concentrate on it and her. She had to have some good inside…deep, deep, deep down. Even if she didn't, he had to save her from herself. That was his job, his honor-bound duty.

However, as she'd asked, who was going to protect him from what he'd just seen and shouldn't want but did?

Chapter Two

Wynona couldn't catch a break.

First Constance had lectured her, then Rafael and now Becca would have her say.

Her office sported more greenery than the reception area, had countless pictures of her and Eric on the cabinet and boasted real Tiffany lamps. The bulbs in those priceless babies flickered at Wynona's presence then stilled, casting colorful light in bright red, sunny yellow, cool violet and deep blue that wasn't as pretty as Rafael's eyes.

He hadn't come back. Maybe that was why Becca had called her in here. Wynona had done what no reaper had before—chased off a guardian angel, aka parole officer, after one super-short meeting.

She should have gloated but was realistic enough to know she might get someone far worse than him. Short, old, ugly and humorless like the last guy. No fun at all. Now she and Rafael... Something inside her fluttered. They'd sparred and shared soulful gazes while feeling each other out. The spark between them was undeniable and might have turned physical. If he hadn't run off.

Becca gestured to her needlepoint sofa. "Please, have a seat."

Sounds like I might need one after our little chat. Wynona remained by the closed door. "I'm good. How about you?"

"Fine." Becca wound a flame-colored tress around her finger.

Her red hair, coupled with her Windex-blue eyes, fair skin and Goth makeup, went well with the silky crop top and harem pants she wore. Tonight's burnished-gold ensemble matched her anklets and toe rings. Definitely not an uptight corporate appearance, though she was still on the far side of friendly given her cautious mood. At least ten feet separated them from each other.

The moment Wynona had shuffled inside, Becca had scurried behind her desk for protection and was trapped now, unless she wanted to escape out of the window to the balcony.

Rather than force her to dive through the glass, Wynona stayed put and got real. "If you need more space, that's cool. I could stand in the hall if you'd like or go back to my office and we could speak by phone. Instant messenger or email works, too. Whatever makes you comfortable."

"I'm good with this." She inched back.

Wynona leaned against the closed door and crossed her arms beneath her breasts. The most non-threatening stance she could manage. If she couldn't touch, she couldn't reap. "What did I do now? Is this about Rafael?"

Becca stopped playing with her hair. "Who?"

So he hadn't come in here and bitched about their meeting, betraying her like so many other guys had. Gratitude and happiness bubbled within her until she recalled that he hadn't returned as he said he would. Her glee disappeared beneath disappointment. "Never mind. Why am I here? Someone else want to see me?"

Hopefully not her newest-new parole officer.

Becca lifted her shoulders. "Not that I know of."

She blew out a sigh and relaxed, kind of. "Then what's this about?"

"Please stop scaring Heather."

Embarrassment and hurt welled within Wynona at being chastised for something that wasn't her fault. She couldn't help what she was any more than a black widow spider could. They and she were born or created that way. "She actually complained about me?"

"Well, no."

"Constance did?"

"Not at all."

"Who then? Wait. Stefin?"

Becca's face turned as red as her hair. "He was concerned."

"About what? Certainly not Heather." She shook with outrage. "He's a pompous SOB. If I could reap him, that sucker would go down like a ton of bricks."

"No need for violence, please." Becca wrung her hands. "I'm sure he exaggerated, and I'm certain you didn't mean to frighten Heather. However, since she is a good fairy, she's excitable. If you could try to tone things down around her, that would be great. Like being careful not to approach too quickly and chill out when she's near. You know?"

"I'm not sure I do. Don't you mean that whenever I arrive here or leave my office, you want me to keep the lights from flickering, the wind from gusting and dogs from howling?"

More warning signals generated by her vibes that told everyone a reaper was close.

Several strays were outside now, wailing like banshees and weres. Every freaking night, the same thing happened. The moment Wynona showed up for work, so did they, along with the wind, announcing her presence to everyone near and far. Didn't help that sweet Heather had taken to feeding the mutts, encouraging them to come back.

Becca stepped closer then retreated the same distance. "We've called a no-kill shelter. They've promised to take care of things."

"Awesome sauce." Wynona restrained her put-on glee. "Who are you planning to call to take care of me if I don't tone things down?"

"I was hoping you would."

"Hey, I can be as agreeable as the next person, but what do you want in addition to me not messing with the electricity, weather and the animal population? By the way, I have no control over that stuff. It. Just. Happens. So do you also want me to be more like Zoe, Constance, Heather and MJ? Is that it?"

"No, not at all." She smiled weakly. "I don't expect you to be exactly like them."

"Whew." Wynona made a show of wiping her brow. "That's a load off. I was worried you'd want me and three naked guys to get it on in the break room like Zoe, Stefin, Taro and Anatol always do. Or maybe steal kisses with a former satyr in the reception area, the same as Heather does with Daemon. That is, when she and MJ aren't strutting around half-naked in their BDSM wear as they try to decide what to wear to a club. Or wait. How about threatening to remove memories from someone as Constance enjoys doing, especially when the person doesn't want that? Or I could be like you, mixing lousy potions and creating spells that never, ever work right for the—"

"I get it, okay?" Becca screwed up her mouth. "None of us is perfect."

"You said it—I didn't. But let me guess. I'm a special case. The other women here don't have to change, but I do, right?"

"I'm only asking you to tone it down a little."

"How?" She uncrossed her arms and gestured frantically. "You tell me. I've always been this way. It's who I am. No one came to me the second I was created and said, 'Hey, Wynona, how about being a reaper? It'll be a blast'." She dropped her hands. "I didn't have a say in this or how I affect things because of what I am. If I'd had a choice, I would have opted for going to prom, cheerleading at football games, having friends, being voted most popular and living a normal life like a mortal or even a socially acceptable supernatural."

She pointed at Becca. "You and the others get kisses and hugs from your guys. Do you know how long it's been since someone has wanted me, other than a reaper or the Horsemen of the Apocalypse? I dated three of those guys at once, all of them turds. Don't get me started on War and Famine. Talk about crappy attitudes. And Conquest? I'm into BDSM as much as the next person, but he went too damn far." She rubbed her forehead. "Do you have any idea what it's like to go centuries without a real hug? Not mindless sex, but genuine affection? Can you even imagine how lonely that gets?"

Becca's face was slack, her color drained. "I'm so sorry. I didn't know…I didn't think. You poor baby."

She raced across the space, arms open. More than a foot away, she stopped and froze before they touched.

Despite her good intentions, there was always the same shit to overcome. Touch a reaper and die.

Wynona hung her head. "I'm not telling you what to do, but your powers will neutralize mine. No way can I harm you, even if I wanted to, which I don't. If you'd like to test things out, touch my shoulder first with your fingertip, see if anything happens. If it does, Heather can always heal you. I swear I'll call her in here, pronto. Then you can fire me. Send me to the shittiest part of Hell. I don't care."

"I'd never do that. And you should care. You don't have to promise anything. I trust you."

Becca threw her arms around her and hugged. Not tentatively, as one would if holding a viper or a corpse. But with tenderness in her caress, care in her heart, one friend to another.

Fighting grateful tears, Wynona embraced her in return, savoring her touch, warmth and sultry scent, totally witchy, completely Becca. "Thanks."

"You're welcome." She rocked them back and forth. "This is only the beginning."

Wynona stilled. "Ah, I don't mean to disappoint you. You're really hot, but I'm not into women."

Becca released her and stepped back. "Neither am I." She gestured to Eric's photos. "I'm talking about the others. Don't move."

She buzzed Heather, MJ, Zoe and Constance.

Zoe arrived first, hair mussed, one tail of her turquoise blouse hanging from her black trousers, the rumpled look courtesy of an unruly client or a quickie with her guys. "Yo."

Becca gestured to Wynona. "Hug her."

Zoe stepped away. "What? Why?"

"She's not only staff and a friend, she's family just as we all are. Go on."

Smoke belched from Zoe's hair. A sure sign she was irritated...or something else.

Wynona cocked her head. "What's the matter, you chicken?"

"I could ask you the same." She inched forward.

Wynona did, too. "Think you're a real badass, huh?"

"Think?" She took another step. "Ha. I *know* I am."

They stood toe-to-toe.

Becca cleared her throat.

Zoe shrugged. "What the hell—I'm game if she is." She held out her arms.

They embraced, each giving their best, and giggled like sisters.

Constance and the others strolled in and got an earful from Becca about treating Wynona like family from now on.

Sounded nice, but before anything happened, Wynona needed to lay out the ground rules for Constance. "During our hug, no touching above my neck to remove memories."

"I'd only target the nasty ones."

"Sadist. Those are the best."

Laughing, Constance eased her close. "You're not going to be alone anymore. We'll always be here for you."

She forced down a swallow and hoped she wouldn't cry. "Same here."

"My turn." Mistress Jin, lovingly known as MJ, prowled close, the bells on her wrists and ankles tinkling. Before she'd become Heather and Daemon's houseguest, she'd lived in his ring. As a genie, she was the poster girl for outrageous sensuality, her long black hair, caramel-colored skin, exotic features, violet eyes and sensational curves adding to her allure.

Never one to be shy, MJ not only embraced Wynona, she snuggled her mound into hers and groped her ass.

Heather made a distressed sound.

MJ returned and slung her arm around Heather's shoulders. "Relax." She shook her. "You know I like being hands-on."

Heather's cheeks reddened but paled fast. She was the only one who hadn't offered a hug.

Her lingering fear wounded Wynona, but she understood. If she'd been in Heather's shoes, she wouldn't have wanted to come anywhere near a lousy reaper. "You don't have to ever touch me. We can blow kisses from across the room and call it a day."

"Like hell." Constance smacked Heather's ass. "Get your butt over there. Nothing happened to us, so nothing's going to happen to you."

"I know." Heather pulled in her shoulders. "I'm ashamed for acting as I have."

"Since when?" Zoe made a face. "You make out with Daemon all the time while we're around and giggle with MJ about fetish wear you two try on in the office. You just now noticed how icky that is? If you want to play, use the break room or a treatment room with the door closed."

"Wait." Constance held up her hand. "I thought she meant holding up a cross to Wynona to protect herself. Even a good fairy should know that crap doesn't work on reapers. Most of the time it does zip for vamps."

"I thought she meant how she apologizes all the time, endlessly, too." MJ took in the entire group before focusing on Heather. "Not necessary, Precious."

"I'm sorry."

"Yeah, we know. Boy, do we know."

"I think she meant not trusting Wynona." Becca rested her hand on Heather's shoulder. "Right?"

"Yeah. I'm so sorry. I should know better. I feel awful. I'm so—"

"No biggie. Everything's forgiven and forgotten." Wynona pulled Heather into her arms and hugged her with all the affection she owned. If circumstances had been different, she would have wanted Heather as her parole officer. Putting one over on the sweet fairy would be a piece of cake.

Mean, too.

Wynona couldn't do that to these ladies. They were her people now. However, when it came to being bad with Rafael, all bets were off.

If he returned.

Rafael sat on the New Orleans Marriott roof, the damp breeze in his face, knees to his chest, emotions running wild. Below, the French Quarter sprawled, alive with good food, boisterous times, depraved thoughts and endless sex. Most of those carnal sensations oozed from the makeover service. Specifically, Wynona's office.

He forced himself to focus on lights sparkling across the mighty Mississippi. The undulating water should have soothed him. Its rolling mass entranced, reminding him of a provocative walk, long legs, tight leather pants and spiked-heel boots tapping invitingly.

He lifted his face to the cloud-smudged sky. The gentle plumes were white as snow, like her hair. Stars winked from the clear areas, their silvery sparkle matching her eyes.

Sweating like the condemned, he squeezed his lids, welcoming the black nothingness. More laughter pealed from the highest floor in the hotel, the sound clear and tinkling. Not throaty or sassy like hers.

He pressed his hand to his forehead. It did zip to remove her from his thoughts and desire. If ever a good angel needed help with unmanageable feelings, he did.

Air rushed over him, warm as life and scented with purity. His supervisor, Frank, had finally arrived. *About freaking time.* Rafael had called for him what seemed eons ago. Although the guy was ancient, even by angel standards, he shouldn't have taken this long to show up.

Frank plopped down, wispy hair wiggling in the breeze. Dressed in a steel-gray jogging suit, he tucked in his wings, a muffuletta in his fist. The huge Cajun sandwich had olive salad, soppressata, mortadella, capicola and provolone stuffed within the roll.

"Sorry I'm late." He took a huge bite and spoke around the food. "Balestrieu's was running a special on these. The line was pure awful. What's up?"

Rafael folded his hands over his throbbing cock. *Maybe I shouldn't have called for help.* Admitting weakness might get him thrown off this case. He'd never see Wynona again unless Satan decided to allow her visits in solitary. "Uh…"

Frank ran his tongue over his teeth and dove in for another humongous bite before coming up for air. "I need more than that."

The exact words Rafael had said to Wynona. She'd answered by swinging her foot toward him. He'd resisted and edged back. She'd followed. Persistent as hell. Sexy as sin. He groaned without meaning to.

"You don't like these?" Frank held up his remaining sandwich. "The smell's grossing you out?"

"No. I mean, yes. No, I mean, no."

Frank eyeballed him. "You working too hard?"

He wasn't doing anything except thinking about Wynona. At the moment, those images were nearly chaste, meaning she still had clothes on in his mind. Give him a few more minutes and he'd have her in nothing except her underwear. He pictured a lacy black bra and an indecent thong, the material so thin perfume would cover her better. "I need advice."

"About what?"

Rafael lifted his shoulders. "Women?"

"You don't seem so sure. You like guys? Perfectly okay. No matter what the folks down here think, paradise is an equal-opportunity lovefest." Frank bumped Rafael's arm. "You should know that by now."

He focused on the Mississippi rather than Frank. "I don't like guys. Not like that."

"Women, either? What do you like?"

A reaper. "Ah, she's a woman. That is, she's female."

"Someone I know? Ursula's had her eye on you since the Dark Ages. She's a looker."

Yeah, if a man wants someone sweet and wholesome. She'd never made Rafael's skin tingle or his head swim during the times they'd hooked up. "Not Ursula or anyone in our circle."

Frank burped. "'Scuse me."

"No prob."

"About your woman problem...we are talking another angel here, right?"

Technically, yeah. Reapers were angels that served Death. Heaven might have equal opportunities for lovers, but there were still class distinctions in everything else. Good angels were at the top, reapers at the bottom since they were considered riffraff. A rebel reaper, as Wynona was, represented the absolute worst. Rafael might as well have coveted Satan's many daughters, all fallen, to top his unspeakable craving for her. "Yeah, she's an angel. As to my work, is there any way to bring a rebel around? Pull out the good that has to be there?"

Frank swiped a napkin over his mouth. "Rebels in general or Wynona specifically?"

He slumped. "She can't be all bad. I don't want to give up on her so soon."

"You've lasted several hours. That's commendable. Granted, most parole officers have made it through a second meeting with her before they questioned their sanity, but hey, we're not looking for perfection. No one expects you to be like Xavier. Tenacious little bastard. He had her for nearly a year. If he'd been mortal, she would've driven him bat-shit crazy. Even with his powers, she gave him a run for his money, but he hung in there."

"How?"

At lightning speed, Frank fashioned his napkin into an origami butterfly and set the design to the side. "Didn't take any of her crap. Put the fear of God into her, literally, so she'd behave."

"Are you serious? I read her entire file, more than five million pages. She offed several mortals while Xavier was in charge."

"Believe me, the carnage would have been far worse if not for his chutzpah. Do double or triple of what he did and those casualties should go way down."

"Have you ever met Wynona?"

"Watched her during a focus group at an executive training session." Frank whistled through his teeth. "You have your work cut out for you. Have fun."

He slapped Rafael on his back and took off, winging his way to Heaven.

Rafael dragged back to the service.

Heather and a beefy guy were kissing behind a fern as though the end of the world had come and they were saying their final goodbyes.

A hoarse giggle tore from the treatment area. Zoe dashed across the hall, her top unbuttoned. The black demon followed in hot pursuit. Stefin and the redheaded guy took up the rear.

Hand in hand, the vamp and the staffer with the hickey left their room and paused to make goo-goo eyes at each other.

Does no one work here?

Rafael gritted his teeth, determined to battle Wynona's most depraved urges. He wouldn't break down, let her corrupt him or drive him away. He'd pull out everything good in her if it drove them both batty.

A buxom redhead in a harem outfit advanced and put out her hand. "Hey, I'm Becca Salt. You must be Rafael. Wynona described you perfectly."

He steeled himself for the worst but also hoped for the best. "Was it a good description? I don't mean accurate. I mean good, as in not nasty."

"You have nothing to worry about. A publicist couldn't have done better."

"Huh?"

"She said you were a total hunk with the most beautiful eyes in the universe."

His legs went rubbery. "Where is she? I need to be with her. I mean, observe what she's doing."

"About that." Becca slipped her arm through his and pulled him down a hall leading away from the treatment rooms. "How well do you know Wynona?"

Not as much as he wanted. He longed to experience her in every way, including a carnal sense...especially that. Saving her from herself was strictly business. "Why do you ask?"

She escorted him into an office with ornate furniture and countless plants. After closing the door, she faced him. "Wynona's had a hard life. Being a reaper is shit, if you'll excuse my French. She didn't ask for it. What she needs is support from all of us here. A kind word. A smile. And frequent hugs. The more the better."

If he did that, there was no telling where his desire would lead. Lightheaded, he sagged against the door. "What?"

"When she performs well, show her. Embrace her like you mean it. A kiss on the cheek, too. Believe me, she'll love the attention and approbation."

Pictures whizzed through his mind—his face buried in Wynona's soft, fragrant hair, lips pressed to her cheek and neck, her top and pants on the floor, his mouth on her breasts, torso, navel and lower, straight to the depths of depravity. "Uh…"

Becca patted his shoulder. "I know it's hard for a parole officer to be hands-on, so to speak. But if you want to pull the best from Wynona, you need to do this. Trust me. She'll respond to affection far more than you being a dick, if you'll excuse my French again."

"No prob."

"She's in treatment room thirteen with a were. Have fun."

That again. Rafael plodded to the room but couldn't go in yet. Hugging Wynona was out of the question. Kissing her wasn't going to happen, either. Too much temptation. However, if he patted her shoulder, shook her hand or smiled then ran like hell, that might get the job done.

After hauling in a huge breath, he walked through the door.

The were was curled in a fetal position on the floor, arms cradling his head. Wynona leaned against the wall, tapping her long fingers against her thigh.

Her leather pants were amazingly nice, but her skin was surely softer.

She glanced over and smiled. Not the cold, screw-you kind, but one that was quick, unexpected and reached her eyes. "Hey, you're back."

She sounded glad. He couldn't have been happier but hid his emotions, mainly from himself.

He joined her, intoxicated by her lavender fragrance and the musky scent of woman beneath. "Hi. What happened with him or it?"

The were moaned. "It's him. I am *not* an animal."

"Fine with me. What's the matter with you?"

"She's gonna kill me and take my soul."

Wynona smiled. "In a New York minute."

Rafael snapped out of his brain fog, his lust replaced by common sense, which she sorely lacked. He leaned close so the were couldn't hear them. "Do you want to go to Hell?"

"Only the good places, like the second circle." She spoke as quietly as he had and met his gaze.

His mind shut off and his libido kicked in, making him sweat from too much excitement. "What?"

She stared at his mouth. "Huh?"

He had to get a grip since she wasn't. "You need to quit misbehaving."

"Why?"

A good question he didn't have an adequate answer to. Relying on his training, he read her the riot act. "Reaping souls isn't allowed for you. At. All. At least, until you're off parole. Then only those you're instructed to take."

"Tell me something I don't know. And before you go ballistic, I told him to get on the table. He refused. For some reason, he thinks if he closes his eyes and can't see me, I'm not here any longer." She rolled her eyes. "If I haul him where he should be, I'd have to touch him. Since he's more mortal than supernatural, that'd be the kiss of death for him. I had no other choice except to threaten. If you know a better way, I'm all ears."

So she hadn't been bad. Yearning battered him again. "Give me a sec." He spoke to the were. "On the table. Now."

"No. I like it down here."

Wynona threw up her hands.

Rafael grabbed the guy by the scruff, lifted him as easily as he would have a feather and tossed him on the table.

Her eyes sparkled. "Whoa, that was legendary. Can you get the restraints on him?" She wiggled her fingers. "Again, if I touch, nothing good's going to happen."

"If you can't get physical with the clients, how can you do this work?"

"I usually handle reapers. Occasionally, I get vamps and zombies, the living dead and the walking dead, so to speak. This is my first were. One of the other enforcers should have been in here to help."

"Where are they?"

"Hiding out."

"Why?"

Humiliation and sorrow flashed across her beautiful face. "They don't like me."

He frowned. "Why not?"

"I'm a reaper."

A damn fine one with hurt in her eyes and an eternity of exclusion in her past. That crap was going to stop now. In a jiff, Rafael had the were strapped in. He glared at the creature. "You do whatever Wynona says from now on and quickly, too, understand?"

"If I don't?"

"I might let her take your soul."

"No shit?" She bounced on her heels.

The were cringed. "I'll be good."

"Wow, you're the man." She patted Rafael's shoulder.

Her touch had more power than a Taser, but in a good way. Heat traveled from his arm to his gut, the warmth pooling in his groin. The pleasure was so intense he could barely breathe. "You were great, too."

"I didn't do anything."

"Exactly. You didn't reap. You restrained yourself."

She beamed. "Yeah, I did."

"Good for you." He pulled her into his arms and buried his face in her hair.

She stiffened then slumped against him. "You all right?"

Her hair was a wonder, amazingly silky, more fragrant than the laws of the universe should have allowed. "A little dizzy."

"Me, too. But I meant, touching me isn't hurting you?"

His cock was huge, the skin ready to split, his balls aching. "Never felt better."

She wreathed her arms around his neck. "Don't stop. Please."

He couldn't if he'd wanted to, and by God, he didn't. Hugging her even harder, he turned her face to his and slanted his mouth over hers.

Chapter Three

The world stilled.

Wynona's longing exploded. She melted into Rafael, desperate to get close, and parted her lips to welcome his tongue.

With a restrained growl, he slipped the sweet thing into her mouth, filling her and exploring, his bristly cheeks rasping her skin.

Her nerve endings fired wildly. Warmth burst within her. Happiness and a thrill she'd never known had her panting for more.

He deepened the kiss, not allowing her one breath or the faintest sound.

Her mind turned to mush. She surrendered, sucking his tongue deeper, adoring his taste — as fresh and innocent as a new day, but also rich and seductive to match the most shameless night. *Crazy good.*

She tugged off the leather cord confining his hair. Freed, those silken locks glided over her hands, thick and wavy, scented with something divine she couldn't quite place. She imagined the scent was how a sunbeam or a shooting star might smell. Otherworldly and unmatched. Yet he was also of this Earth, a passionate being, no different from her.

Indulgence was on their menu. Control not allowed.

She buried her fingers in his mane, hopped into his arms and wrapped her legs around his lean hips.

He teetered from her weight but righted himself easily like the strong guy he was. All lean muscles rippled with power, biceps and shoulders bunching, cock thickening. His rod wiggled against her cleft.

To show her gratitude, she moaned for all she was worth. His tongue muffled the base noise, which transformed the sound into a softer, more feminine response. Already, he'd conquered her and she didn't mind. He could freaking tame her as much as he wanted during moments like this.

He cupped her ass and turned a slow circle. A sensual dance she couldn't resist. From the second she'd come into being, she'd yearned for intimacy fueled by lust but also laced with tenderness.

Rafael supplied the precious emotion in spades. His kiss was less frantic now, more searching, reaching beyond the façade of her leather outfit, outrageous bravado and smartass comments to the real woman beneath.

Lonely, wanting, horribly insecure.

Unease flickered through her. Walls went up. Submitting to carnal hunger was one thing, craving anything beyond that was certifiable. She was a reaper, lowest of the low, more hated than politicians, lawyers and used-car salesmen.

This had to stop.

Rafael wrapped his arm around her waist and coaxed her closer.

Fevered and reckless, she pushed his tongue from her mouth and filled his with hers.

He groaned heartily.

The door flew open and smacked the wall. Shoes slapped the linoleum. Foul-smelling sulfur hit. "Stefin here."

Wynona couldn't have cared less. She cupped Rafael's face and kissed him hard.

Stefin sighed. "I see she's attacking you, just as I feared. I warned you about getting rid of her, but did you listen?"

Rafael sucked her tongue deeper.

The were's restraints rattled. "Hey, you, Stefin, unbuckle me." The were jiggled his fasteners and moaned. "They both threatened me. He's going to let her take my soul."

"Relax. For a small fee, I can protect you."

"Screw that. Additional fees aren't in the contract."

"Then get ready to die. Your choice."

The were growled.

Stefin clucked his tongue. "You disappoint me, Rafael. How could you have let her corrupt you so easily?"

Rafael stilled.

Before Wynona could get him back in the mood, he pulled his mouth from hers and let go. She held on like a clingy fool who didn't want the good times to end. He, on the other hand, was ready to ditch her without a second thought or a first regret because of Stefin's stupid comment.

If Rafael believed these last minutes had corrupted him, his head was going to explode when she really got down and dirty.

Stefin circled them. "Do you want me to pry her from you? It would be my pleasure."

"Go on." She smiled sweetly. "I dare you."

He rocked on his heels. "You don't think I will?"

"Not unless you'd enjoy a few months in traction."

"That's enough, both of you." Rafael pulled her legs off him.

Her heels hit the floor with a whack, jarring her bones. Tottering backward, she pulled him with her. He pried her arms off him, then put as much distance as he could between them.

His color was high, his eyes glazed and his hair deliciously mussed, those dark waves grazing his shoulders. During their kiss, she'd released several of his shirt buttons. Each time he breathed, the fabric pulled apart, revealing his chest. Nothing except smooth, bronzed skin, sculptured pecs and abs.

Her knees sagged.

Stefin gestured to Rafael's shirt. "Better get decent. Becca gets pissy whenever she sees skin, even if it's during our breaks. Closing the door doesn't matter, either. Believe me, I've tried. Go figure, huh?"

Rafael's face flushed from red to maroon. He fumbled with the buttons, his hands shaking so much he couldn't get them to work.

"Let me help." Wynona crossed the room to him.

He danced away. His ass and shoulders passed through the wall. On the other side, a creature wailed. Rafael jerked back into the first room and pointed at her. "Stay where you are. Not one step closer."

Her cheeks burned. She lowered her hands. "This good enough or would you like me to go to the next building? Possibly the next state?"

"You can't leave now." Stefin tapped his watch. "Not time for your break."

She leveled her gaze on him. "Do. You. Mind?"

"I already said I did—weren't you listening? I'm not going to do all the work while you're gone."

Only a sack of rocks could be denser than him. "Beat it. I want to be alone with Rafael."

"Oh, yeah?" Stefin glanced past her. "Better make it fast. I think he's about to black out."

Ashen, Rafael cleared his throat. "I'm good."

He sounded turned-on, his baritone ultra-deep and breathless.

She couldn't haul in enough air either. "Stefin?"

"What?"

"For the last time, leave us alone."

"Tell me how that's possible with the were still in here."

She'd forgotten about him and had blocked out his endless bellowing. "Knock it off or you're history."

His cries died in his throat.

Rafael finished with his buttons and straightened his collar. She'd shoved it down to touch his neck while they'd made out. His stony features said he wasn't pleased.

That wasn't the reaction she required. Before he'd come into her life, she'd been lonely. Now, she was uncertain, too. "Let me make a wild guess—you regret kissing me."

He lifted his face and lowered it just as fast, ignoring her to smooth his clothes. He paused on his fly, flushed and tugged up the zipper.

She'd been a bad, bad girl. Despite her earlier doubt, he had enjoyed every second she'd been in his arms, no matter how he acted now. Her beard-scoured cheeks and his taste on her tongue and lips were the proof she needed of his desire. Still, his current behavior disturbed her. She wanted to make certain that guilt, not something else, had caused his reaction. "Can I ask you something?"

He didn't meet her gaze. "No matter what you do, I'm not going to resign as your parole officer. I intend to watch you closely and ride you exceedingly hard."

She stroked her cleavage. He couldn't seem to look anywhere else. "Yeah? Promise? Especially the riding hard part?"

He shoved back his hair and ogled her thighs. "I'm going to work you hard. Here. In this service."

"That'll do, too."

He glanced around the floor and frowned.

She swiped his leather tie from behind a chair. "Is this what you're looking for?"

He reached for the thing.

Their fingers touched.

A jolt more powerful than the Big Bang coursed between them.

He shuddered.

She trembled. "Tell you what. We could talk about your plans for me in my office. I'll throw the lock so no one disturbs us."

He snatched the cord and put more distance between them. "No."

Stefin tapped her shoulder.

She turned on him, teeth bared. "What?"

"A little advice. He's not that into you."

She elbowed Stefin away and focused on Rafael. "I still need to ask you something."

"Not now."

"When?"

"Later."

"How much?"

"When we're alone."

That could be on the far side of never. "No can do. You're obviously unsettled by what happened, so I have to wonder, why did you kiss me first?"

"Wait, wait, wait." Stefin waved his hands and spoke to her. "He did you before you did him?"

"Yep."

"You're sure?"

She gave him a look that said he was a dumbass then pointed at the were. "You. What happened in here?"

"Now you want me to talk?"

"Either that or scream when I push my fist down your throat and rip out your soul. Up to you."

"That's not going to happen." Rafael stood in her way. "Your rebel reaping days are over. Especially here." He frowned at Stefin. "I kissed her first, all right?"

Stefin's eyebrows shot to his hairline. "No shit?" He scrunched his face. "I don't understand. Are you seriously that horny? You don't get any in Heaven?"

Wynona pinched her nose.

Rafael yanked down his shirt cuffs, checked his specs and patted his pockets.

That hurt worse than when he'd peeled her off him. "I steal souls, not glasses or smartphones, so there's no need to see if anything's missing. Getting back to my question... You still haven't answered."

He rubbed his temple.

"You've already forgotten what I asked? Need me to repeat it?"

"No. Becca and I had a talk. She told me to kiss you."

"What?" Stefin gaped. "She bitches at me, Zoe, Anatol and Taro for doing what comes naturally, but for you two it's all right?" He crossed his arms and tapped his foot. "That's not fair."

Didn't make sense, either. "Our Becca said that? The half-witch who owns this place? Or is there another Becca in Heaven who oversees you riding female reapers exceedingly hard?"

Rafael clenched his jaw. "Your Becca told me to praise you when you did well. To offer a hug and a kiss so you'd feel good about yourself."

A punch to the gut couldn't have hurt more or been as demeaning. Wynona staggered back. "And good boy that you are, you simply followed her advice."

He averted his gaze.

What the fuck's that supposed to mean? I'm right? Wrong? Not even close? "Look at me, dammit."

He did, for a split second. "You behaved yourself and didn't kill and reap that." He gestured to the were.

The guy showed his teeth. "I'm not a *that*. I'm a *him*, okay? How hard is that to remember?"

Rafael shoved his hands in his pockets. "I was supposed to show you how pleased I was at your work performance, so I did by hugging and kissing you."

Not because he genuinely liked and wanted her. Tears welled in her eyes. She blinked them away. "I want another PO. Now."

He stared.

"Get out of here." She pointed at the door, the walls, the ceiling, whatever way he wanted to leave. "Don't ever come back."

He didn't budge. "You're not the one who makes those decisions."

Of course not. That would be too fair and easy for a crappy reaper. White-hot hurt leached from her, replaced by an icy chill and resolve. "Fine. Stick around if you want. But I'm warning you, stay out of my way. Don't look at, talk to or dare touch me again. If you try, I will make every second of your existence seem like the bottommost pit of Hell, and that will be on a good day."

She stormed from the room.

Rafael wasn't sure what had happened. One minute, Wynona had been in his arms, her lips as soft as a sigh against his, her breath warmer than new life, her scent fresher than spring. In the next, she'd been biting off his head and spewing one vile threat after the other. Each oddly sexual and completely enticing.

His rod stiffened even more, making it difficult to walk. Despite the hurt and the danger she'd threatened him with, he had to follow her...but only as her PO, nothing else.

The moment he reached the door, Stefin stepped in front of him. "Great job." He clamped Rafael's shoulder.

He stifled a gag at the demon's sulfur stench and gritted his teeth at the searing heat from his hand.

Stefin leaned close. "You got rid of her faster than I'd ever dreamed possible. If I'd known it would be this easy, I would have kissed her first. As head of the enforcers, I should have."

A snarl erupted from the hall.

Stefin flinched and spun around.

Zoe couldn't have looked more murderous, hair smoking, flames soaring in her eyes.

Stefin folded his hands and lowered his face. "I was just kidding about the kiss. I'm not that brave."

"Good thing." She arched one eyebrow. "What about being head of the enforcers?"

He sighed. "That, too. You're the manager and in charge here."

"Of what?"

His face colored. "All the enforcers, including me."

"What about when we're home?"

He growled. "We both know who runs things there."

Her cheeks got rosy. She looked down the hall. "What happened with Wynona?"

"That wasn't my fault. Rafael kissed her and she took off. Could be for good."

Zoe glared at Rafael.

He stepped back. "I was simply following orders."

"Whose? Wait." She shot daggers at Stefin. "Yours?"

"Not me, I swear. I came in while they were doing the deed."

Rafael made a face. "We were simply kissing. It was Becca's idea. She said to hug Wynona and kiss her if she did a good job. She did, so I did."

Stefin nodded. "He told her that, too. Made it perfectly clear he was only kissing her because he had to."

Zoe regarded them as she would a creature with three heads. "Are you two for real?"

Rafael lifted his shoulders. "I'm not following."

"Clearly. Stay away from Wynona, understand?"

"How? I'm her PO."

Stefin slung his arm around Rafael's shoulders. "Wynona asked for another parole officer but he stood his ground. Good man." He shook him. "He has every right to mount and use the reaper whenever he wants."

Rafael breathed through his mouth and tried not to wince at Stefin's scalding heat. "That's 'ride and work her at her job'."

"Same difference."

"Not to a woman." Zoe grabbed Rafael's shirt and yanked him into the hall. "Cool your heels in the break room. Do not leave there until one of us tells you to. Stay away from Wynona until we can undo what you've done. If you're lucky, you can be in the same room with her in a month or two. Being able to talk to her will probably take longer."

"What?"

"Hey, you're the one who screwed up. Don't except us to work miracles."

"I was simply following orders."

"Yeah, yeah, yeah. Move it."

He backed away, cut the corner too short and passed through the wall.

Heather and MJ looked over, both nude except for thick leather bands around their waists and upper thighs, the items decorated with silver buckles and zippers. Fetish wear he'd seen in Wynona's file.

He wanted to scream. "Does no one work here?"

Heather scrambled for her clothes.

MJ grinned. "Not unless we have to. Wanna stick around and watch us try on this stuff?"

Heather slapped MJ's arm and sucked in a breath, her vivid blush fading. "Sorry. I shouldn't have hit you, but I don't want anyone looking at me like this except Daemon. And you."

"And the people here and the ones at the clubs we visit. Can't forget about them."

"That's different. He's my guy, you and I are BFFs, like I am with Becca, Constance and Zoe. At the clubs, we don't have a choice. If we don't wear this stuff, we can't get in. So this is okay in those instances. Not with him." She lowered her voice. "He's a stranger."

"Not if he keeps coming back."

"True, but until then we can't invite him to watch. Still, I was out of line to smack you. Please forgive me. I didn't mean—"

"I know you didn't. Come here." MJ hugged her. "How about we try the orgasmic belts next? I hear they're a blast."

They giggled.

Rafael slogged to the break room. Sprawled in a chair was the guy who'd made out with Heather earlier. All muscle, he looked well over six feet, had sun-kissed skin and dark brown hair long enough to skim his shoulders. Crumbs clung to his bristly upper lip. Chocolate smears dirtied his mouth. Strewn across the table were Hostess cupcakes, Milky Ways, Milk Duds and several bulging sacks from McDonalds.

He shoved a whole cupcake into his mouth and swallowed without chewing. "You're new."

Rafael had never felt as old as he did now. He sank into a chair.

"Taking your break? I'm Daemon, by the way. Used to be a satyr until I ditched my hooves for feet. They're ugly as hell — my feet, not my former hooves. Becca used Eric's as the prototype. What can I say, least they work. The best part of me is my cock. Heather makes me cover it when the pizza guy delivers. She doesn't want him to feel bad because he's not as hung as I am."

Rafael covered his eyes with his hand.

"Don't worry, I wasn't going to show my stuff to you. Wouldn't want to hurt your feelings, either."

He groaned.

Cellophane crinkled. Paper ripped. Daemon belched. "Want a cupcake? I don't usually share, but I only have two minutes to eat the rest of my snack before I'm back on the clock. Don't know if I can finish that fast. Here."

He slid a cupcake to Rafael.

Heather popped in, fully dressed. "Daemon, no."

He froze. "What? I didn't belch. Okay, I did once, but it didn't bother him. He was okay as soon as I promised not to show him my rod. I did good, right?"

"Perfect. Except for this." She put the cupcake back on Daemon's side. "No sharing with him. Not after what he did to Wynona."

Rafael held up his hands. "I didn't do anything I wasn't supposed to."

Daemon pushed a Quarter Pounder into his mouth, swallowed and stifled a belch. His nostrils flared. "What happened? Did Stefin put you up to something? He's had some damn cool ideas about the reaper. Shooting her off in a rocket. Digging to the center of the earth, dropping her in and building a skyscraper over the hole. Blindfolding then shanghaiing her to the far corners of the universe without a map so she can never find her way back."

"Stop it." Heather smacked his shoulder. "Please." She stroked the spot she'd hit. "Rafael kissed her."

"Get out. You're a brave man. Some might say crazy, considering."

Rafael bristled. "Because she's a reaper?"

"Isn't that enough?"

"Maybe you people should be nicer to her. In fact, as her parole officer, I'm insisting on it."

"Nicer, like kissing her as you did?" Daemon's cheeks puffed out. He slapped his hand over his mouth. "Sorry, but even the thought makes me want to hurl. Hanging out with MJ is bad enough, but a reaper, too?" He shuddered.

Rafael frowned at Heather. "You're the good one here. Tell him to be nice to Wynona."

"I'd like to, really."

"Then do it."

She sucked her lower lip. "How nice?"

Poor girl's as clueless as the others here. "Verbally nice, not physically. No need to kiss or touch, ever."

If any guy was going to enjoy Wynona, it'd be him — long, hard and thoroughly.

The room whirled. He gripped the table and lowered his face.

Heather touched his shoulder. "You okay?"

No. The effects from his and Wynona's kiss had returned with full force. Her glorious touch, the way she'd sagged against him. Not because she had to. She hadn't seemed able to help herself.

He'd lost control just as easily. Part of his reaction was naked lust, but the greater portion was a longing to be close, connect and lose himself within her stunning heat, her incomparable fragrance.

Too bad all that cool stuff belonged to a rebel reaper. Worse, his charge. He'd had no right to overstep his bounds with her. He should have made her lush ass off-limits, ignored her precious nipples poking his chest and kept their French kissing to a minimum. No more than a couple minutes tops. What had he been thinking?

Heels clicked in the hall. Becca stopped in the doorway.

Daemon shoveled food into his mouth with both hands. "I'll be through in a sec."

"No rush. But would you mind finishing at Heather's desk? I'd like to have a word with Rafael alone."

He slumped. Now, Becca would come down on him when the hugging and kissing had been her idea.

Heather and Daemon cleared out fast.

Steeling himself, Rafael waited for the worst.

Becca closed the door and sat next to him. "I heard what happened. How could you? I mean, you're supposed to be one of the good guys. You and I talked. I practically begged you to understand the situation. So how could you?"

"How is this my fault? You told me to hug and kiss her, which I did, just as you said."

She narrowed her eyes. "I told you to kiss her cheek, not shove your tongue halfway down her throat."

He didn't recall her saying anything about a cheek, just the kissing.

She snapped her fingers close to his face.

He leaned back. "What are you doing?"

"Trying to get rid of your lewd grin."

I was smiling?

Becca scowled. "When did I tell you to hurt Wynona's feelings by saying the only reason you kissed her was because I told you to?"

"Never. But in my defense, she did ask."

"You couldn't finesse your answer a little?"

"I was caught up in the moment."

"Yeah, I heard. You guys were spinning like a top with her legs around you and your hands on her butt."

Heat rushed to his face. "She would have fallen if I hadn't held on to her. She could have gotten hurt."

"She *was* hurt. By you." Becca poked his chest. "Now she's not talking to any of us, especially me. She thinks I set this up so you could make a fool of her."

"What? No. I'd never. I like her." *Too damn much.* Hadn't he proved that with his outrageous kiss?

Becca stood. "You have a funny way of showing your feelings for a woman. For the next few days, keep your distance. I'll have Zoe provide you with a report of what Wynona does during her shifts. You're not to approach her in any way, shape or form. I don't care what your orders are from on high. This is my turf and you'll abide by my rules while you're here." She backed way. "I have enough trouble running this place without you adding to my problems or making one of my friends feel bad."

"Sorry."

"Save your apologies for Wynona, if she ever talks to you again."

Chapter Four

She was back to being a stone-cold reaper and got icier with each passing day. *Screw being nice and having friends. To hell with hugs and kisses.* Wynona had lived without that stuff for eons. She'd manage to get through her time here, no matter what anyone did.

Suddenly, the staff members were born-again sweethearts, no longer diving into treatment rooms to avoid her as they had in the past. Locks weren't thrown, gazes weren't averted. If they smiled any harder, their damn faces would crack.

Becca must have told them to play nice. *Too damn little, too pissing late.* Wynona wasn't impressed.

A vamp sauntered into the hall accompanied by a female staffer who sported more hickeys than moles. They cuddled then froze upon seeing her.

In the past, the staffer would have bolted. The vamp might have hissed to show his masculine and supernatural superiority. *Dumb turd.* Today, they flashed edgy grins, remained rooted to the spot and even lifted their hands in greeting. The staffer's palm was damp, probably from the vamp's slobbery kisses.

Wynona breezed by without bothering to glance their way. Although being on the receiving end of contempt was murder, as she well knew, experience had taught her that indifference was far worse and the most horrible response one person could give another. It reduced the recipient to nothing. That was what she intended to employ now for everyone here. No matter what it took, she'd keep her peace and wait for the day when she could reap at will without anyone, especially Rafael, haunting her every move.

These last days, he hadn't spoken to or dared touch her. However, he always managed to get to an area first then cut out before she arrived, leaving his fragrance in the halls, by Becca's office, in the reception area and the break room. No matter how hard Wynona resisted, she kept catching his celestial scent, pure wonder mingled with sheer bliss and utter male.

Each time she smelled him, her legs wobbled so much she had to sag against the wall to keep on her feet.

Earlier in the week, he'd exited the break room and halted at her sniffing his scent like a rutting dog on the prowl while bracing herself against the wall so she wouldn't drop to the floor.

Her face had burned in embarrassment and lust.

His had colored, too.

They'd stared at each other and the rest of the world faded away.

Until Zoe had rounded the corner and stopped dead. Her caution had said she'd expected them to kiss and make up, or rumble. If they'd done the latter, he would have gotten the worst of it. Wynona wasn't a punching bag for anyone any longer.

Pulling herself together, she'd pivoted, ambled to her office and closed the door gently even though she wanted to rip it off its hinges and cry. Hating herself for being such a pussy, she'd curled up in her chair and watched *Grey's Anatomy* online. The characters' fucked-up lives had nearly made her forget her own.

After that, she'd breathed through her mouth whenever she'd been away from her office so she wouldn't smell Rafael in the air. Wasn't a hell of a lot she could do about her eyes though, except close them so she didn't see him again.

That proved impossible.

Yesterday, she'd pulled a Pepsi from the break room fridge, taken a sip, turned and nearly choked. He'd been in the doorway, blocking her. His expectant gaze had told her he'd been waiting for her to say something.

She hadn't been able to. Her throat had been too tight to speak. Her pain still too raw.

Daemon had barreled inside for his snack and had practically knocked Rafael off his feet. '*Hey, sorry. Didn't see you.*'

Rafael was bigger than life and all that registered in her brain.

Daemon had made a beeline for the junk food Heather had left on the table for him.

Seizing her chance, Wynona had sped by Rafael without a word, glance, growl or kiss.

Never had she felt more bereft or empty.

Twice more, he'd popped up unexpectedly during her shift. The first time, she'd needed additional forms from Heather. While she'd collected them, he'd also come to the front desk.

Heather had gone even whiter than normal then blushed scarlet.

Wynona had suspected the poor thing didn't know whether to be fearful or embarrassed as to what might happen.

Nothing would. '*Thanks.*' She'd grabbed the papers, strode away and ducked into the ladies' room. Each stall had proved empty. She'd contemplated masturbating to take the edge off but had dismissed the notion as absurd. Only Rafael would do between her legs.

During their second encounter, she'd been hurrying from a treatment room. He'd been striding down the hall. They'd nearly collided. He'd reared back immediately. That had hurt like a sonofabitch because he hadn't wanted to risk physical contact, possibly because she'd warned him not to. Since when had he listened to her wants and needs? She still hungered for his embrace no matter what a prick he'd been.

He'd smiled, almost as though he couldn't help himself.

Her misgiving had faded. She'd drunk in his long, dark hair, exquisite eyes, full mouth, bristly cheeks, broad shoulders, sculpted abs and the precious bulge between his powerful thighs.

It had risen to the occasion, pressing against his pants, trying to reach her.

Her grin had happened before she knew it. She'd wanted him to say hi or something, anything so they might get past this awkward stage, scream at each other as lovers did then make up with wild monkey sex.

Becca had entered the hall.

He'd spun around and walked through a treatment door. The vamp in there had hissed.

Rafael hadn't come out, preferring to be with a bloodsucker rather than her.

She'd slunk away and swore that if it killed her, she'd forget him.

Thereafter, he'd made himself scarce. The staff, however... She drew them more easily than a corpse attracts flies. Whenever she was with a customer, there always seemed to be an audience watching closely, cheering her on.

Waiting for me to fuck up?

She guessed Zoe or Stefin reported her every move with clients to Rafael.

Maybe it was time to give her PO something shocking to hear or read. After holding back for too long, she was ready to cut loose tonight.

She marched to the reception area. Lights flickered, dogs howled, wind rattled windows.

Heather flinched, but her grin didn't waver. "Thanks for taking this client."

A reaper. What else? His dark suit was perfect for a funeral director, his complexion pastier than the Pillsbury Doughboy's, his features skeletal, hair colorless and lank. He was the spitting image of what mortals thought reapers should look like. During the Dark Ages, they had adhered to the vile appearance. By the time her model had come along, everyone knew a reaper could get more souls by being attractive rather than gruesome.

He took in her leather bodysuit, cut low on top and snug everywhere else. With her four-inch heels, she towered over him.

He stared at her boobs that were in danger of falling out if she breathed too deep.

"Hey there." She stepped closer, hips swaying. "I'm Wynona." She slapped her hand on the back of his neck and tugged him in to her. "What's your name?"

Heather choked and coughed.

He glanced at Heather then back. "Ah..."

"Take your time." She stroked his onyx tie. "We can get acquainted in your treatment room."

With her arm hugging his waist, she moseyed down the hall, her hip bumping his ribs.

He cleared his throat. "You're a friendly one, aren't you?"

"Are you complaining?"

He gawked at her breasts. The mounds bounced merrily with her steps. "Will mortal babes be like this with me after I go through the program?"

Only if he had massive plastic surgery and came out looking like Rafael. *Fat chance of that.* Becca would probably have to call her mom, a celebrated witch from a respected coven, and get her to whip up a cosmetic potion. Not that this dude's new appearance would change anything. He'd still be a reaper. "You do understand that with mortals you can look but not touch, unless you're claiming them forever."

"Totally. But it would be nice to have them running after me for a change rather than me having to chase them while they shriek, sob and pray that I go away. Does shit for my ego."

She understood where he was coming from and yanked him closer. "I'll do my best to see that you're not only utterly satisfied, but deliriously so."

"Wow, this is some service."

"You haven't seen anything yet, but I swear you will."

Stefin, Taro, Anatol and Zoe looked over. They huddled by the reaper's treatment room. Wynona suspected they were tonight's audience. So be it. She'd put on a real show for them. Once Rafael learned the particulars, he might sprout some gray hairs.

Let him feel like a loser for a change. Dismissed. Unwanted. Forgotten.

Zoe bared her teeth, her attempt at a smile. Taro and Anatol slapped on their friendliest faces. The stuttering flames in their eyes told the truth. They still feared or disliked her. Stefin arched one eyebrow and glared.

Zoe drove her spike heel into his foot.

His eyes rolled into his head. Once he'd recovered, he offered a pained smile.

Wynona steered the reaper to the doorway and cupped his scrawny ass, making certain everyone saw what she did. "This way, hon." She directed him into the room and squeezed his butt.

He shot to his toes. "Damn, that feels good. Can you give me something to make mortal women do that?"

"Sorry, no. They can't touch you, either, unless they have a death wish. But I can help you relax."

"I'm horny, not uptight."

"You will be once the program starts. Let's nip those nasty feelings in the bud." She spun him around and hauled him close, their thighs touching. "No tongue, understand?"

"What?"

"Quiet." She claimed his mouth.

He jerked, parting his lips.

She clenched her teeth, pinched the skin on his ribs and twisted hard. He moaned, clamped his mouth shut and played dead, the same as a virginal bride.

Precisely as she wanted. He wasn't the world's worst kisser, but no freaking way would he ever be Rafael. His mouth commanded. His lips embraced. His tongue conquered and satisfied.

Damn him for making her yearn. Tears stung her eyes. She squeezed her lids tighter and hardened her feelings. Rebels didn't bawl like little girls with broken hearts. They got through the worst crap and did more than survive. They thrived.

She cupped the package between the reaper's legs. Pure awful. Flaccid and wanting.

He gasped. So did someone else. Given the gravelly sound, it had to be Zoe. Frantic whispers followed.

Good, Wynona had shocked them, including the reaper. He got over his surprise quickly and pushed his meager stuff into her palm. Not because he liked her. He wanted to use her for relief then take off for more deserving babes, just like all guys.

Not this time or ever again.

She released him and stepped back. "On the table."

"Whatever you say." He undid his tie, pulled it from his collar and looked at her questioningly.

"What?"

"After I'm naked, did you want me to help you finish undressing?"

Her right boob hung free from when they'd kissed. She stuffed it inside the leather. "I'm keeping my clothes on since I'm on the clock."

His mouth turned down. "Does that mean you're through relaxing me?"

"Damn straight." Zoe snapped her fingers and gestured Stefin forward. "Your turn to take care of our client."

Stefin stared. "You expect me to kiss him?"

The reaper skittered back.

Zoe rubbed her temple. "No, you don't have to kiss him. Get him on the freaking table like you would any client."

"Got it." Stefin rolled his shoulders, unbuttoned his cuffs, folded them back and made fists as big as hams.

The reaper pressed against the wall. The little color he owned had drained from his face.

Zoe gave Wynona her sweetest smile, which would have curdled a mortal's blood. "You did an awesome job escorting the reaper here. Best I've ever seen. Right, guys?"

Taro pumped his fist and whistled through his teeth. Anatol applauded. Stefin grunted.

Zoe tapped her foot. "What was that?"

He wrenched the reaper from the wall, picked him up by his throat and dropped him on the table. After smoothing down and buttoning his cuffs, Stefin gave Wynona a stiff grin. "You did great."

"Oh, yeah?" She eyed him. "You know what that means, at least according to Becca. Now you have to hug and kiss me. The rest of you guys, too." Wynona opened her arms. "Come to mama."

No one moved.

Smoke rose from Zoe's hair. She batted it away and exhaled noisily. "I hate to pull rank..."

"No prob." Wynona got kittenish. "If you'd like to hug and kiss me first, I'm cool."

The flames in Zoe's eyes flashed. "Do you want Rafael to send you to Hell with no chance for parole?"

She shook her head. "Who?"

Zoe frowned. "Your PO."

"Who?"

"Look, I know he hurt your feelings."

"What are you talking about? I don't have any. I'm a reaper. We're lower than radioactive sludge." She spoke to the client. "Right?"

He leaned away from Stefin. "I'd say we're way below that."

"Not to us." Zoe edged closer to her. "We want to be your friend. You're my sister. My family. Becca's, too, and everyone else here."

Sounded nice, a regular fairy tale in fact...as in too good to be true. "I'd prefer coworkers who keep their distance and don't put on a show because they think I'm too stupid to get it." She pointed at the guys. "If any of you dares praise my work again, says anything nice or smiles even once more, I'll make certain you regret it."

Stefin chuckled. "How? It's not like you can yank out our souls since we don't have any."

"I can rip off another part of you. One that will really hurt. Can't I?"

Taro and Anatol covered their groins and stepped back, sober as pallbearers now.

Zoe shook her head.

"Why are you still here?" Wynona glared. "Shouldn't you be racing to wherever Mr. Wonderful is to tell him about my behavior today? When you give him your oral or written report, make sure to mention my kiss with...uh..." She turned to the reaper. "What's your name?"

"Olaf."

Poor guy's hopeless. She focused on Zoe. "Make sure what's-his-name knows about my time in here with Olaf, how nice I'm treating clients and that after my shift, I'm going to be equally friendly while I party hearty at an area nightspot."

Olaf tapped her shoulder.

She whirled around. "What. Is. It?"

He held his hands to his chest. "Do you mind if I come with you?"

"Free country." She turned back to Zoe. "Did you get everything I said or would you like to use the computer in here to key in details?"

The flames in Zoe's eyes faded to pinpoints. Her hair stopped smoking. "Please don't reap anyone. Don't put yourself in unnecessary danger just because you're still hurt."

Wynona's throat constricted. She wanted Zoe to hug her but wouldn't ask. Weakness was for sissies or fools who enjoyed getting steamrolled by life, mortals, supernaturals and hunky male angels. No way. For her, those days were over.

"I'm not promising anything." She brushed past and stalked to her office.

* * * *

Rafael rolled his forehead over the break room table, arms dangling by his sides. The latest report on Wynona had hit him harder than he'd expected. If that wasn't bad enough, Anatol, Stefin and Taro had added juicy verbal details to the facts, making a terrible situation worse. To his relief, they'd stopped jabbering a few seconds ago, but kept a silent watch on him now.

Daemon massaged Rafael's back, his touch clumsy and rough, but at least his hands weren't boiling hot like the demons'. "You doing okay?"

Like Heather, Rafael couldn't lie. A cross good angels and fairies had to bear. "No."

"Maybe this is for the best. Reapers belong together. While Wynona and Olaf are out tonight, what can she do to him?"

Make him a man, put color in his sunken cheeks, stiffen his limp rod and pull delighted screams from his shrunken chest when she should be doing those things to her PO. The guy who was supposed to call the shots with her.

He hadn't a clue how things had gotten to this point.

For two weeks, he'd been a good soldier and steered clear, not saying a word about the increasingly disturbing reports on Wynona. How she was now taking her breaks on the balcony, which attracted howling mutts from miles away. When the breeze picked up, she wouldn't budge from the spot until she'd generated hurricane-force winds. Several buildings around there needed new roofs. Once inside, she'd strolled down hallways on the lower floors, playing havoc with those patrons' lights.

Since her in-your-face behavior hadn't done any real harm, except for some repair work, he'd resisted cracking down, afraid she'd hate him more than she already did. Thankfully, she'd been professional with the clients, until tonight. When had the makeover program included fondling Olaf's sagging ass, cupping his puny balls, welding her mouth to his thin lips and practically inviting him to join her as she prowled the nightspots for other conquests?

Not souls. Oh, no. Tonight, she'd be on the lookout for reapers, vamps or zombies who'd let her crawl all over their bods while she did the nasty to them.

An anguished moan poured from him.

"Feel good?" Daemon massaged harder.

Pain slashed down Rafael's back. He grabbed Daemon's wrist. "You can stop. Thanks." He sat up and sucked in air.

Taro, Stefin and Anatol exchanged a glance.

Rafael panted at the lingering hurt. "What?"

"Wynona's clearly losing control." Stefin rested one arm on the table. "So why not give her enough rope to bury herself?"

"You mean hang herself?"

"Same difference. Let her run wild and get into all sorts of shit. Then waltz in, pick up the pieces, throw her in a dungeon and move on to a new case. You might get a bad fairy the next time. I hear they're way easier."

"Don't count on it." Daemon snorted. "You haven't met Heather's adoptive parents. Rotten to the core. Last time she begged them to come to the apartment they ate all the food and blamed the empty refrigerator and cupboards on me, even though I was here working. When I pointed that out, they said I hauled the stuff here and that they were starving to death and would sue me if they ended up in the hospital." He stuffed two Hostess cupcakes in his mouth and talked around them. "I should be so lucky."

Anatol nodded sympathetically. "Thank God Zoe doesn't have any relatives. Did Heather's folks go to the ER and send you the bill?"

"They tried, but MJ got rid of it fast. Redirected it to them with added charges she put on there. They fled the state. Heather's bummed about that, but hey, I say good riddance—"

"Ah, guys?" Rafael slumped in his chair. "Can we get back to my problem?"

They looked at him blankly. Taro scratched his throat. "What was it?"

He squeezed his fists to rein in his frustration. "I can't give up on Wynona. I know I can save her. I have to. It's my job." The truth, sort of. He wanted to turn her around for reasons that had nothing to do with his position. He wanted to be near her.

Her shift had ended ten minutes ago. Without saying goodbye to anyone, she'd fled as if the office was on fire, Olaf close on her heels. "Where would she go for a nightspot?"

Taro lifted his shoulders. "There are dozens of places in the area, maybe hundreds catering to supernaturals."

"Try thousands." Daemon peeled off the wrapper on his Milky Way. "You need to count clubs she could fly or teleport to."

Rafael shook his head. "Not possible. She's earthbound until she serves her full parole or I discharge her early for good behavior." He knew that wouldn't happen. "When SACS learned about her rebel reaping, they took away her clearance and clipped her wings."

The flames in Stefin's eyes danced. "Ripped those things right out of her, huh?"

Rafael made a face. "No. Her wings are still there. She simply can't unfurl them."

"What kind of punishment is that?"

"We're not medieval up there. The rack's been in mothballs for a long time."

"Not in Hell it hasn't. Some of my best times have been on it at the BDSM clubs in the second circle."

Anatol and Taro nodded.

Rafael rested his head in his hands. "You guys have to help me. Think. Where could she have gone tonight? What's close enough to this place for her to have walked or run to?"

"Wait." Anatol scooted his chair closer. "She left with Olaf, right? Are his wings fucked up too? If not, he might have flown or teleported her far, far away."

That would make locating her like trying to find a needle in the proverbial haystack. They could have gone to countless universes. SACS was crazy for not having insisted she wear an ankle monitor. "Did she look like she liked him enough to take off on an extended trip?"

Taro slid the report to Rafael and tapped the folder. "It's all in there. She was really coming on strong."

Bile rose to his throat. He swallowed it down, labored through the report a second time and relaxed, sort of. Despite the guys' breathless rendition of what had happened between Wynona and Olaf, their kiss had lasted mere seconds, not minutes as his and hers had. She'd stuffed her naked boob back into her top rather than letting Olaf suck her nipple. She'd claimed she had to stay dressed because she was at work. *When does a rebel reaper let rules get in the way of having fun?* She must have been putting on an act with Olaf, which meant she'd gone to a club under her own steam. Unless Rafael was kidding himself. "When she smiled at him, did it reach her eyes? Did she moan softly when his tongue was in her mouth? Did she wiggle her pussy against his rod?"

Dead silence.

When he'd first entered the break room, they couldn't wait to blab about what had happened. Now they were mute. He clenched his jaw. "Did she do any of that or not?"

"Not that I saw." Stefin shrugged. "But I don't look at her unless I absolutely have to."

"You wrote the report. Clearly, you watched her tonight and I still need to know if she really liked him or if she was simply pretending to."

Anatol slung his arm over the chair. "You mean to make you jealous?"

He hoped. That would mean she cared rather than hating him completely, or worse...being indifferent to him.

"Hold it." Stefin slammed his fist on the table. The wood cracked. He turned to Taro and Anatol. "Remember when we first met Zoe and she told us hands off when it came to her?"

Taro slouched. "I've been trying to forget those dark days."

"Me, too." Anatol brushed his dreadlocks over his shoulder. "It was pure murder. First with Becca insisting we not use our powers so we could suffer like mortals do and learn some humility, which meant no money, fun, raising hell or sex. Then the problem with Zoe. Fuck."

Stefin smiled. "But things got way better when my Zoe came around."

"Not *your* Zoe." Taro lifted his chin. "She's ours, too."

"Only when I allow it."

Anatol chuckled. "Dream on."

"Guys." Rafael rapped the table. "My problem, remember?"

Stefin frowned. "That's what we're talking about. We pissed off Zoe by claiming our rights as men to rule her as we should. For that truth, she treated us badly. We, in turn, ignored her. What shrinks call reverse psychology. She couldn't stand it and pursued us as you're now pursuing Wynona. I get where we were coming from. But you? I can't imagine want you see in her."

Fun. Sass. And, oddly enough, yearning as deep as his. She was like no woman he'd ever met, which added to her charm. "If you couldn't use your powers in the beginning, does that mean you guys never went anywhere but here and your respective homes on foot?"

They laughed.

No one follows the straight and narrow any longer. "I take it you did cut loose after hours. Where exactly?"

"The Crucible."

They'd answered as one.

Rafael stood. "Point me in the right direction."

"Hold on." Stefin tugged him back down. "You can't go there."

"Why not?"

Anatol made a sweeping gesture taking Rafael in. "You're a good angel. One whiff of your righteousness and the patrons would scatter like roaches in a spotlight, never to return. The management wouldn't like that."

"So?"

"If Wynona's there, she wouldn't appreciate you showing up and messing with her good time. Do you plan to drag her out of the place?"

"I thought we could talk."

"Like you do here?"

Rafael ground his teeth. "What do you suggest?"

"A disguise." Taro glanced at the others. "He could watch her without her knowing. If she does anything wrong, such as kissing Olaf like she means it or humping him like there's no tomorrow, Rafael could slap on the cuffs, haul her out and have his way with her."

His cock thickened. He resisted the pleasurable feeling. "Or I could talk to her."

Their loud laughter filled the room.

They were completely loony, but he had little choice except to ask for their help if he wanted to save Wynona from herself. "What kind of a disguise? What would I go as?"

"Definitely someone less uptight." Anatol pursed his lips. "You're positively corporate in that getup. The cord needs to go first."

The leather tie jerked away and flew across the room on its own. Rafael's hair swung forward, wiggling from an unseen force. When his locks stilled, he risked a touch. His do was fluffed up and tangled as it would be if he'd cavorted with Wynona.

Before he could indulge in the wicked fantasy, his brown pants morphed into black leather, the crotch tight enough to crush his balls. Wincing, he tugged to give them more room. His ivory shirt transformed into black silk. Instead of buttons, the garment laced in front, the wide V it created showing skin from his pecs to his navel. The training films in Heaven hadn't shown anything this decadent for men. Not even those for Chippendales dancers and they were the worst. "You expect me to wear this in public?"

"What else?" Stefin spoke to the others. "Should we put makeup on him, too?"

"What?" Rafael leaned away. "No."

"The glittery kind kicks serious ass." Daemon swallowed four Milky Ways at once and burped. "Heather has some killer blues and greens. She stashes them here just in case we get an urge to visit a BDSM club. I'll get them from her."

Rafael grabbed Daemon's wrist. "Don't bother."

"I don't mind."

He did. "No makeup. None of this, either." He gestured to his costume. Referring to what he wore as clothes would be too kind. "I refuse to let anyone see me in this."

"Why?" Stefin winked. "You look so hot."

Taro and Anatol bent over laughing.

Rafael held back a shriek. "How would all of you like to go on parole with Xavier calling the shots?"

Taro snickered. "He couldn't be any worse than Becca."

"Fine. I'll get her in here and see what she thinks."

"Sit down." Stefin gestured Rafael back to his chair. "We've been yanking your chain, all right? However, you do have to wear that to blend in. With us surrounding you, no one will notice what you really are."

"You're coming, too?"

"Trust me, you may need protection. It's sleazy as hell there."

Taro grinned. "Happiest place on earth."

"Especially tonight." Anatol wiggled his eyebrows. "Half-price drinks for females. There'll be tons of guys eager to pour whatever they can down the ladies' throats. Get them nice and relaxed for a night of loving."

Rafael shot to his feet. "Come on, get dressed. There's no time to waste." Wynona was likely there with Olaf and possibly hundreds of other lust-crazed goons.

Anatol, Taro and Stefin didn't move.

Taro shook his head. "Dressed?"

"Yeah, like me." Rafael tugged on his crotch. It didn't help. His groin and legs were so sweaty the leather adhered to him like glue.

"We can go in with what we have on." Stefin gestured to their black shirts and pants. "We're regulars. Even if we weren't, the flames in our eyes are a dead giveaway for a demon." He pushed up from his chair.

The others followed, except for Daemon, who slapped his hands together, ridding them of crumbs.

Rafael didn't want him to feel left out. "Would you like to come, too?"

"Another time. Heather and I have plans. MJ will probably tag along as she always does."

Stefin slung his arm around Rafael's shoulders. "Let's go."

Faster than a blink, they left the break room and entered what Rafael guessed was the Crucible. Metal guitars squealed, drums pounded, banshees screeched lyrics from the small stage, each creature ugly as sin, their killer bods clad in black leather and lace. Mega-loud music shook the walls and glasses. Smoke plumes pressed down from the ceiling. Numerous patrons screwed on the tables and floors.

Rafael gaped and turned away, thankful Wynona wasn't involved in such depravity, at least with a guy other than him. Someone smacked his hand. He spun around.

Stefin bounced his shoulders in time to the foul-mouthed tune and said something Rafael didn't hear.

"What? I didn't get that."

"Decent crowd tonight!"

Rafael cringed at Stefin's bellow and the music. A little louder and his ears would bleed.

"Hey." Anatol tapped Rafael's shoulder and pointed.

The smoke and crowd parted like the Red Sea. Tucked within the frenzy were Wynona and Olaf, sharing a table. Rafael's mouth went dry. He pushed through the crowd before he realized he was doing so.

She and Olaf weren't making out as he had feared. They weren't touching at all, talking to or even looking at each other. Despite the crowd, they were in a circle of emptiness, most likely because they were reapers.

He hurt for her and wanted to growl at the goons here for making her feel lonely and unwanted, the same as Stefin and the others did at work.

Her face was down, shoulders slumped, her mood forlorn.

Tenderness flooded him. He ached to give her a hug and so much more.

Seemingly unaware he was watching, she nursed her Death in the Afternoon, a potent drink combining absinthe and champagne, the mixture created by Ernest Hemingway, who would have probably loved this place.

She let out a prolonged sigh, glanced over at Rafael and stilled.

He wanted to smile but wasn't certain he should. She might misunderstand and think he was making fun of her being with ugly Olaf. He wished they could talk like regular people, rather than a PO and an RR doomed to be at odds with each other.

She turned in her chair then squinted, zipping her gaze over him. She regarded his hair again before checking out his eyes. Her mouth fell open.

Call him crazy, but it seemed she'd just recognized him...or thought what he wore was as dumb as he did.

He lifted his hand in greeting.

She tightened her jaw.

Disappointment gripped him. He'd hoped for softness, the same that she showed him when they ran into each other in the hall and the break room. No such luck tonight. However, the sole way for her to flee, without powers, was the door behind him. Unless she had enough strength to ram through the wall.

He held his breath and waited, prepared to catch her if she bolted past.

She pushed from her chair and crawled on the table.

If she planned to leap over him, no biggie. He still had his wings and could fly up to catch her.

On her feet, she danced, bumping and grinding to the music, wiggling her booty in Olaf's face. He grinned. Even for a reaper, he had a disgusting smile.

Rafael shoved two vamps aside so he could get to her before they did.

She threw back her head and wailed in time with the banshees, her hips undulating, boobs bouncing.

He stopped at the table, transfixed.

Wynona dipped, swayed, spun. Lavender and musk rolled off her and caressed him. His need mounted, his cock pressing against his balls, both hungry for a loving caress.

Olaf reached for her.

Rafael punched his hand away.

The reaper shrieked.

Too bad. Wynona was Rafael's to save, protect and guide.

The guitars twanged one last deafening time. The banshees fell silent. Other sounds filled the relative quiet—heavy breathing, kissing and fucking.

Wynona slowed and looked down, defiance in her eyes.

Damn, she was something. He offered his hand.

"Hey." Olaf stood. "She's with me."

Rafael didn't take his eyes off her, afraid she'd run or disappear and never come back. He hoped she wouldn't reject him. She had every right. He'd treated her badly without realizing how awful he'd been, more worried about his own turmoil than her feelings.

He prayed she'd be a better person than he'd been.

With a sigh that might have been pissed or weary, she slid her fingers over his. Her touch was supercharged, delivering riotous pleasure and heat, the promise for more. There had to be more.

He helped her down.

Once on her feet, she pulled her hand from his and backed away.

He followed. Nothing else was possible.

She stopped and lifted her chin. "You look ridiculous."

"I know."

Her frown faltered. "Why the costume?"

He nearly smiled. Although they were at different ends of the angel spectrum, at times they did think alike. "To get in here."

"Why? This isn't your type of place."

"I know. I came to see you."

Her caution lessened then returned full force. "You could have seen me at the office, all day, every day."

"You told me not to."

She shifted her weight. "Why?"

"You were pissed, and rightfully so."

Her eyebrows inched up then sank back down. "That's not what I meant. Why did you want to see me here?"

"To talk. Actually, to ask a favor, if you can agree."

She edged back. "To what?"

The truth he couldn't deny any longer and had known from the moment he'd first seen her. "I want you to corrupt me."

Chapter Five

Wynona's vision dimmed. The room twirled. Swaying, she clutched the first thing she could.

Olaf patted her fingers that she'd dug into his bony arm.

She jerked away and staggered back. Weres, bad fairies, warlocks and shifters scattered before she could touch them.

Rafael alone followed her.

His hair was a cloud of dark temptation, deliciously mussed, his leather pants ungodly tight. Even in the gloom, his ginormous erection and plump balls were obvious. Their musky fragrance hit her with tsunami force, the scent rich and decadent.

She teetered again and drank him in.

Perspiration clung to his powerful chest, the heavier drops rolling to his navel. Short dark hairs circled the depression and arrowed lower, beneath his waistband.

She'd lied. He didn't look ridiculous. He was the most magnificent creature she'd ever seen and had surely gone bonkers. Or he was trying to trick her so she'd leave without a fight.

She searched his eyes, afraid of what she'd see there.

Heat and need blazed within, as deep as hers.

Her breath caught. She stumbled back.

Rafael advanced, pursuing her as no man had.

She bumped into someone. The clammy cold said he had to be a vamp, his chill seeping into her.

Warmth poured from Rafael, inviting her closer, proving Christmas had come early this year and not only because she genuinely liked him. For the first time in forever, she was about to get what she'd wanted for so long — a chance to corrupt a PO and hold his fall from grace over his head. Once the deed was done, he'd have no choice except to let her reap at will, cull the herd, take down any fucker who hurt women or dared to look at her the wrong way.

Too many had. She was as welcome as the plague, her past horrible, present worthless, her future a black hole with no lasting friends, family or love. The ladies at From Crud to Stud had tried to like her, but they'd eventually snap back to reality and would loathe her like everyone else did.

Rafael included. He'd learn how vile she was and would then turn his back on her and hook up with a good angel who shared his philosophy. A woman he'd love and respect.

There wasn't a chance in hell she would live through that. She fought hurt and tears. "What is the matter with you? Have you lost your goddamn mind?"

Despite the blaring noise, several patrons glanced over.

Drums pounded, metal guitars twanged, the banshees howled their newest song. Attracted to the coarse beat, the crowd boogied again, forgetting the drama surrounding her and Rafael.

Stefin, Anatol and Taro strutted her way, as though they had the fucking right. She gave them the finger. They stopped and kept their distance.

Rafael eased closer, sorrow in his eyes. "You don't want me?"

He couldn't be serious. She craved him more than an opportunity to be the popular girl who'd found Prince Charming and a McMansion at the end of her rainbow. "You have no idea what I want."

"Tell me. I'll listen."

Of course he would. He's perfect. She sagged.

"What is it? I'm not your type?"

If she'd been a sentimental fool, she would have believed he'd been created just for her.

He gave her a puppy-dog look that cut right to her core. "I'm not good enough for you?"

She smacked his shoulder. "Now you're talking crazy shit. How much have you had to drink?" He had to be wasted. Booze or drugs were the only explanation for his outfit and behavior. Most likely a prank Stefin and the guys were playing on him at her expense. They wanted to see her squirm.

Before she let that happen, she'd claw out their eyes. She leaned close and sniffed Rafael, expecting to smell liquor or pot.

Two scents bombarded her — one fresher than the dawn of time, the other more wanton than her X-rated thoughts, his angelic and male fragrances combined. Longing tore through her so ruthlessly she nearly cried out.

He stroked her hair. "I didn't come here to drink, dance or do the other stuff everyone's engaged in." The couple at the next table screamed introductions to each other then fucked like crazy. He reddened. "I came for you."

That couldn't be possible. "Have you forgotten you're my PO?"

"I'm a man first." He touched her wrist.

Her breath caught.

"Forget about the other stuff, please. I have."

She threw her arms around him, powerless against her feelings but also worried about his. It wasn't like a good angel to behave this way. He looked drug-free and lucid, except for his weird request to be corrupted. It was always possible Stefin and the guys had swiped what Becca called her 'magic for dummies' book and cast a spell or given him a potion so they could have a few laughs at the effects. Unless they'd had another demon possess him. "We need to talk. No, wait. We have to get out of here first."

He wound his arm around her waist. "Hold on."

Beneath the music and crowd, a familiar rustling sounded.

He unfurled his wings, each more than twelve feet long. Every woman knew what a wide wingspan and large hands meant on a man.

Patrons ducked or skipped back to avoid those babies hitting them.

She trembled at his gorgeous feathers, which were so white they shone. Unfortunately, this wasn't the best place to show them off. Reaper wings were black. Only good angels had ones like his.

A dangerous rumbling ran through the crowd. The hunkier demons and supernaturals looked like they wanted to brawl.

She bounced in place. "Better file your flight plan and take off."

Rafael held her more firmly, his colossal erection snuggling against her pussy.

Bewitched, she clung to him.

He flew to the ceiling.

"Hey." Olaf glared from the floor. "You're leaving?"

Poor guy wasn't only homely, he wasn't too swift, either. "Hold it." She gripped Rafael's shirt. "I can't go through walls or ceilings any longer. SACS cut my power."

"Not a prob. You're with me now."

Indeed, she was. Effortlessly, they slipped through plaster, wood, insulation and shingles to the outside. The breeze swept past, cool and moist, not yet gusting from her presence. Trumpets wailed sensually. Laughter rang out. Conversations rose and fell.

No one looked up. Rafael had made them both invisible to man and beast. Stray dogs lifted their muzzles and sniffed but finally gave up and searched the ground for her scent.

He soared upward, away from the wind's grip. Stars twinkled above them. Lights shimmered below.

Wonder filled her. The last time she'd experienced such freedom was when she'd been able to fly and teleport. She hadn't realized until now how much she'd missed her powers. She should have been pissed at SACS for every cruddy thing they'd done, yet couldn't help embracing this small slice of happiness. It wouldn't last. Never did. "Where are we going?"

Rafael's irises glinted, the blue shockingly beautiful. "To talk."

"At your place? Heaven?"

He stopped ascending and hovered instead.

He really needed to work on his body language and poker face—his discomfort was far too obvious. He didn't want her in paradise. Who could blame him? Taking her there was no different from a crown prince introducing his druggie girlfriend to his mum, the Queen.

Rafael lifted his shoulders. "Your place?"

She hadn't straightened up before leaving for work, but what the hell, it was either there or a treatment room at the service. "It's not much."

"I don't mind."

He wasn't putting her on. Not because good angels couldn't lie—his tender caress and touching smile spoke volumes. They really had to have a chat. "Do you need directions?"

"No." He banked west to her place. "The address is in your file."

Of course it was. She'd forgotten he was her PO. Blame it on how he'd dressed and behaved tonight, currently nuzzling his colossal rod against her cleft. If she got any wetter, she'd embarrass herself and prove what a silly fool she was.

A badass reaper would have given him the cold shoulder at the club, raised hell then run like mad when he'd tried to take her into custody. She'd caved faster than a pre-teen in the throes of her first serious crush.

When will I ever learn?

She rested her face against his neck, her nipples poking his chest.

His cock got harder than reinforced concrete, maybe even steel. A woman could get hurt from such awesome masculine power.

She gripped him even tighter.

They neared her Victorian apartment building, a pink-and-white confection with ornate moldings, a widow's walk and lacy ironwork balconies. No need to tell him she rented the attic. He already knew and made a perfect descent into her place.

She didn't bother to turn on the lights. The moment he touched down, her cheapo lamps flickered wildly from her presence and finally settled, casting the cramped space in a dull yellow glow.

Rafael's wings slid inside his back. He turned a slow circle, taking in the discipline straps hanging over her lone chair, one- and two-headed dildos on her shabby nightstands, crops, whips, manacles, chains, slave collars, masks and other BDSM stuff scattered throughout the room.

His cheeks colored, but he didn't glance away or bolt. He focused on the brass bed, her nicest furniture. A lavender-and-black satin comforter bordered with ecru lace covered the king-size mattress.

She was a romantic at heart. *So sue me.*

Before he could comment on the enigma between her soft side and her obvious depravity, she pushed the chair into his legs. He dropped into the seat.

She paced, stepping over her stuff. "Before you left the service tonight, did Stefin, Anatol and Taro give you something foul to drink?"

Confusion darted across his face. "No, why? Does my breath smell?" He blew into his hand and sniffed.

She tugged his arm down. "Relax. There's nothing wrong with your breath." She examined his eyes.

They widened. He blinked. "What are you doing?"

"Checking for demonic possession."

"What?"

There wasn't any. No flames wiggled in his eyes. The blue was more beautiful than she recalled. "Did the guys say weird words over you and wave their hands or a wand or chicken feet or something?"

"Are you all right?"

"Me?" She stepped back. "I'm not the one who came to the Crucible and asked to be corrupted. Someone must have put a spell on you."

"You did." He reached for her.

She danced away. It was the hardest thing she'd ever done, but his future was at stake. For herself, she didn't care what happened. "Whose idea was it to go to the club tonight?"

"Mine. I asked the guys where the closest joint was that you could walk to and they took me there. Before you ask why, it's because I wanted to find you and be with you."

So she could corrupt him. "You can't possibly want this."

He glanced around. "Would you rather we go to a hotel?"

"What?"

"If you don't want to stay here, we can —"

"I'm talking about your corruption. Stefin must have put you up to this. Maybe you forgot or misunderstood."

"I may be a good angel, but I'm not brain dead. He and the other guys did their level best to convince me to get rid of you and ask for a bad fairy as my next charge. I told them no freaking way. I wanted you and only you." He bunched his shoulders, fisted his fingers and thrust out his bottom lip.

A little more of that from him and she'd be in love. "You do realize how wrong our screwing around would be? Downright depraved, in fact. Once we've finished, you will have gone where no good angel has before. You are aware of that, right?"

"I was counting on it and more."

She shook his shoulders, hoping to snap him out of this lunacy. "Good God, man, what's gotten into you?"

"You. How many times do I have to tell you that?" He hauled her onto his lap, her legs straddling him, her pussy touching his balls and cock. Heat rushed from him into her and warmed Wynona faster than Satan's hellish depths ever could. Rafael was beyond hard. His kiss more than wicked, well past debased.

Where did he learn this? What does it matter?

She savored his unparalleled taste, lost in their passion. These last weeks without him had been worse than lonely. The endless hours had been cruel. She'd never expected much from existence except endless reaping, along with a few laughs and some mediocre orgasms.

Being in his arms went beyond her wildest fantasies. Which this was. Drowning in his lust wouldn't change reality. He'd be out of her life longer than he'd ever be in it. What they were doing wasn't worth the trouble or grief.

She couldn't let go.

He cupped her ass, stood with little effort and strode to the bed. The frame groaned from their combined weight, the mattress shimmied and her breasts popped out of her top. He latched on to one nipple and squeezed the other.

Too many feelings rose to the surface—desire, happiness, fear, confusion, sorrow and need. She pushed the bad shit aside and concentrated on the good. This represented a once-in-a-lifetime chance she didn't want to miss. Paradise couldn't be better unless he was there with her, smiling, scolding, sharing and loving.

Not possible. They only had now.

She tugged his shirt, wanting it off, him nude and inside her.

He lifted his head, eyes dazed, lips damp. Without comment, he swooped back down and sucked her neck, tickling her.

She giggled. "Take off your clothes."

He panted, his breath warming her throat. "I thought you liked my costume."

"I prefer skin. I want to see yours. I want to see everything."

His clothes flew in all directions, his boxer briefs landing on her lampshade, his shirt on the floor, its laces torn away, back ripped. He'd also broken his fly during his enthusiastic striptease. On his knees, he faced her.

Her belly fluttered.

His tiny nipples were the same color as fine cognac, pecs and abs nothing but hard slabs of bronze muscle. Dark, silky hair peeked from beneath his arms. Male fur trickled in a thin line from beneath his navel to his groin, and his cock jutted from thick black curls.

He was even larger than she'd imagined, simply exquisite, his meaty crown scarlet with passion. Pre-cum shone dully on the slit. Ropey veins snaked up the thick column. Short dark hairs dusted his succulent balls. His powerful thighs and calves were wonderfully hairy, too. All man.

He searched her face. "You like?"

"Are you kidding? You're drop-dead gorgeous."

He smiled self-consciously. "Now you. I want to see every part, nothing hidden."

She put out her hand, stopping him from touching her. "Not so fast. You're not done."

He glanced down at his nudity then over at his clothes. "I took off my shoes and socks."

"You did, but I want to see everything."

"What else is there?"

"Show me your wings, and I'll show you the way to Hell and back."

Laughing, he unfurled them. Thankfully, her room was wide enough that the tips stopped before touching the walls. She pressed her hands to her chest. "Wow."

He flapped them and flexed his cock.

"Now you're showing off."

"You know me too well."

She didn't know him at all but wanted to, desperately and foolishly.

He stroked her thigh. "Your turn. Please. I've been fantasizing about you for weeks. I tried not to but couldn't help myself. No, that's not right. I didn't want to stop. Thinking about you was the only thing that made my days bearable."

All the praise in the world couldn't have touched her more deeply than his sweet confession. He wasn't someone who could con to get what he wanted. The truth meant something to him.

Humbled by his desire, excited too, she tugged off her boots and struggled with her bodysuit zipper, breaking it as he'd done with his. Slowly, she peeled off the leather, oddly shy that she hadn't worn underwear. His approval of who she was as a woman and a reaper meant the world. Maybe it shouldn't have but she couldn't be that dishonest with herself.

Acceptance shone in his eyes, along with enchantment. He beamed.

Heartened, she pitched her bodysuit past his left wing. The garment landed on her whips.

He took in her breasts, mound, eyes, mouth then journeyed back to her cleft. "I had no idea anyone could be so perfect."

"I was aiming for the chair."

"You know what I mean." He gestured from her head to her toes. "Perfect."

"No, you're wrong, I'm not." Millions had proven that by avoiding her. "I'm a reaper."

He smiled. "Oh, yeah."

His enthusiasm touched her in places that had gone dead long ago. Now, his unconditional esteem threatened to bring them back to life. Wynona wasn't certain she could survive such joy. She'd definitely spiral into lasting darkness once he left her side, which he would. A relationship between them could never last. Reality didn't work that way. "You might want to kill your zeal. Being a reaper isn't good."

"You want to debate this and lose? You will with me. Or do you want to move on and enjoy ourselves?"

She kissed his hand. If they'd been standing, she would have knelt to him. Every god on Earth could have taken lessons from him on how a man should behave with a woman. "I'm all for making love not war."

Grinning, he pushed her onto her back, spread her legs and pressed his face to her slit.

Her breath spilled out. His whispered over her damp folds, his mouth possessing yet also honoring. Rather than rush or use her as though she were nothing but a warm body, he licked her cleft lovingly. No one had ever done that. Reapers mated like Tasmanian devils. Vamps were into stinging love bites. Zombies were dead meat with crappy personalities.

Rafael clearly knew what she desired, even if she claimed souls.

Each teasing stroke registered within her entire being, releasing something deep inside. Perhaps it was hope, she didn't know, but bliss finally broke through and flooded her with sweet anticipation. She wiggled into him, eager for their intimacy even if it was only physical. Maybe it would prove enough.

He stopped licking and sucked instead then slipped his finger into her channel. She squeezed those muscles. After easing a second finger inside, he slid them in and out. She surrendered and lost track of everything except this. Her world reduced to his presence, scent and touch.

He delivered pleasure at a leisurely pace, building her carnal need in small steps until it had reached an unsustainable level. Heat congested her pussy and tension followed, coiling, mounting, driving her over the edge. She thrashed more than the dancing patrons had at the Crucible. An epic climax pummeled her. A pulse beat deep inside her channel.

Gulping air, she sprawled over the mattress.

He lifted his face. "You okay?"

She sucked in another breath and blew it out. "Never been better."

"Seriously?"

"You're the man."

"Not yet, but I will be."

He scooted into position, grabbed his cock and thrust deep, filling her to the brim and then some.

Her mouth sagged open. His did, too.

God, he's adorable. "Come here." She cupped his face and brought his mouth down to hers, tasting herself on his lips. Strange yet nice, though not as wonderful as his flavor, which was the best ever. Afraid she'd never get enough, she speared her tongue inside.

He grunted but let her run this part of the show. As for the rest... He pumped, a slow slide in and out of her as he'd done with his fingers. His rod was immeasurably better. Thick and hard, stretching her mercilessly with her full consent.

She pitied the self-righteous, who considered sex dirty or shameful. *Why bother to be alive if one can't indulge in this? With the right man, of course.*

Who would have guessed her perfect mate was a good angel? Not her.

She kissed him harder and deeper, reckless with desire and weakened by need.

He thrust, his strength barely restrained. Their bodies smacked. His wings bounced and created a cooling breeze. She smiled. So did he, their mouths still joined.

At last, he broke free and gulped air, his face and throat sweaty. Hers were, too.

On a thunderous growl, he rubbed her still-sensitive clit. She bucked, taking his cock deeper. He shuddered but didn't stop, pumping faster and harder, forcing her back to the precipice.

Wynona fought him. She didn't want to come again, at least not yet. Maybe in a day or two, possibly a week. They could play hooky and call in sick. If they got in real deep shit, they could share a dungeon in Hell. Anything was possible. Hell, he was actually here and doing this.

He thumbed her nub without pause, relentless in what he wanted to do.

She resisted, pushing her feelings aside, becoming stone again. No way would she come until she was damn good and ready.

He licked her nipple.

She shattered and soared. Tension peaked then drained away, leaving her shaky and floating. Her sheath pulsed around his shaft and sucked him even deeper, every rigid inch.

He hadn't gone soft. Either good angels never did or he hadn't come.

Still panting, she parted her lids.

His hair pointed in every direction. His face was a grimace, complexion close to purple.

"Good God, what are you waiting for?" She squeezed his arm. "Come before you explode."

He gritted his teeth. "In a sec." He eased out and plunged back inside.

Wynona's silky heat was more than Rafael could withstand without coming, coming, coming. He couldn't yet. He had to draw this out for minutes, hours or days.

Forever if he could...

So much moisture drenched her channel his head nearly blew off. Her boobs were spectacular, nipples dusky, skin pale and flawless. He'd expected white curls between her legs to match her hair. She didn't have any down there, her cleft naked and vulnerable, her pink folds puffy.

Nothing in any universe could match.

With so much to look at and do, he wasn't going to last longer than another few seconds before he climaxed. His legs trembled. His arms were about to give out. He'd already sweated off five pounds or more.

Ursula had never done this to him.

With Wynona, he couldn't catch his breath, the room kept swirling and his peripheral vision was gone. This was better than dying and reaching Heaven.

"Come!" She beat the mattress. "Now!"

He rubbed her clit to keep her from rushing him and nagging.

She jerked and screeched. "No. I can't take this again, dammit. I'm still sensitive from the last two times."

And I'm not? Even his wings were super receptive to any touch. His cock had already lost control. One more thrust and he'd be a goner, deflating faster than a saint's hope for world peace. No way could he give in so fast. Wynona deserved the best ride ever and he damn well intended to give it to her.

He grabbed her calves and hauled her feet over his shoulders.

She choked on a cry, coughed and stared. "Wow. You're better than the man."

"Not yet." But he would be.

He pumped jackhammer quick. The headboard banged into the wall, creating a hellacious racket.

She gripped his forearms. "Don't worry about the neighbors."

"I wasn't."

"Good man. Please, don't stop."

Never, not with her.

He brushed her clit. She lifted her chin and wailed. He shifted to get even deeper and plowed into her with a fanatic's fervor...or a man who'd finally found what had been missing from his existence. Someone precious and required.

She seemed so young now, downright defenseless, even though he knew better. She could take down a whole city at once, claiming everyone's souls. Thank God, she hadn't. Even Satan would have buried her deep and thrown away the key for having caused so much havoc.

Rafael would never have known these moments. Without them, how could he exist?

He thrust again, liking how her boobs wiggled. He gave her nub a few seconds' rest then got back to business, rubbing her quickly. She gasped, squirmed and tried to pull away from his hand. Impossible. They were together now. He was in too deep and didn't intend to change that.

She whimpered.

He smiled.

Growling, she squeezed her cunt rapid-fire around his rod.

He gasped in surprise and stupefying lust but held off. Barely.

She fought her climax the same as he did, both trying to make the other come. A contest he hoped would end in a tie, with each winning. If not, he might be the first angel in history to die from too much joy. His shoulders and arms throbbed. His knees wanted to give out. If his balls and cock could have wept and begged for relief, they would have.

His sac tapped against her ass, deepening his frustration. Every time she squeezed his shaft, he wanted to wail but didn't have enough air to do so. Keeping conscious was a monumental effort.

She tugged her hair and swore.

The expletives sounded sexy coming from her.

He got harder.

She yelled and climaxed, face red, skin damp, eyes wild.

Her orgasm hadn't happened a second too soon. Using his remaining energy, he pumped savagely, sensing she'd like that.

She beat her fists against the mattress. "Yes, yes, *yes.*"

He smiled at her happiness, gasped at his own climax and bellowed, control and respectability gone. Euphoria he'd never experienced barreled through him, leading to a place he hadn't known existed. Sinfully good, decidedly right, totally perfect.

Woozy, he lowered her feet to the bed, sank down and propped himself on his elbows to keep from crushing her.

Wynona's face had more color than he'd ever seen. Her hair was tangled and damp, lips bruised from their kisses. Her lids were at half-mast but her eyes sparkled.

He pecked her mouth and hauled in another breath. "Am I still the man?"

"Better. A freaking god."

Not even close, but she had brought out his beast. "Thanks. Sleepy?"

"Hmm." She'd already closed her eyes.

"Wynona?"

She breathed evenly. Her head sagged to the side.

His spirits sank. He wasn't ready to be alone. He was eager to talk, laugh, share and love, but he didn't want to disturb her.

With his shaft still inside her sheath, he folded his wings over them, providing more privacy and warmth, then he settled down to nap.

Chapter Six

Wynona had faked sleep, not knowing what to say after the best lovemaking ever. What she and Rafael had shared wasn't mindless sex. Their smiles and teasing, the way he'd folded his wings to protect them, had made the moments surprisingly intimate.

When other supernaturals had drilled her, it had been always been wham-bam, thank you, ma'am with no thought as to cuddling afterwards. They'd taken off for their next conquest or had passed out, not caring what she thought or felt.

She was used to that. This... Her emotions were too raw and unruly now, those feelings uncertain where to go or what her moments with Rafael might mean. Laughter, tears and fear raged at the same time.

He was too good for her. A hard notion to admit, but them hooking up would ruin him. If SACS found out about tonight, he couldn't bend or break the truth as she always did to wiggle out of a bad situation. He'd confess, apologize and would most likely beg for punishment because he was too decent. That was his fatal flaw. A little white lie never hurt anyone. Once his supervisors learned the truth, they'd surely clip his wings. She didn't want to consider what else they'd do to make him an example, but those worries pressed close.

If they didn't consider his indiscretion too awful, he might get nothing more than confinement in Heaven where he'd have to subsist on ambrosia and nectar for a while, their version of bread and water.

Should they really be pissed at him, he could face a demotion, like being reduced to a fallen angel and banished to hell, or worse... He might end up as a reaper like her, forever doomed to take on the shit jobs in the universe, which meant being reviled by every culture, feared by innocents and condemned to the sorrow she'd always known.

She tensed to force back panic and squeezed her eyes to stave off tears.

No way could she let anything bad happen to him. She had to lay down the law and convince him a relationship between them was suicidal.

Only how?

He wasn't one to heed good sense. He'd proven that by showing up at the Crucible tonight dressed in those ridiculous duds. She suppressed a giggle at how cute he'd looked, then she spiraled back into anxiety. Pretending she hated him or he hadn't pleased her in bed wasn't an option. At some point, their sexual gymnastics had yanked the comforter and sheet from a corner of the mattress. Her lampshade listed to one side, possibly from his wing hitting it. His cock was snuggled against her cleft, dampened by his seed and her moisture. She'd never been as wet. His chest crushed her breasts. Her nipples poked him. No way would he believe this hadn't turned out mega great. He was a good angel, not an imbecile.

Maybe if she told him she was into women more than guys...

He'd never believe it after tonight.

She could say she'd only slept with him so he'd get off her back, figuratively, concerning her rebel reaping. If she put on her best act, she could make him feel like a total fool for having believed she enjoyed him as a man.

The thought made her ill. To diminish him in any way even to save his ass wasn't something she could do.

Round and round she went, searching for an answer.

Something popped. A sound she couldn't quite place. Another pop.

Mystified as to what had made the noise, Wynona rolled over, surprised she could do so. Rafael's weight no longer confined her. Her sheath was empty, or rather abandoned as it usually was.

Relief should have washed over her, but she couldn't lie that well to herself. Afraid to open her eyes and learn he'd left without even saying goodbye, she patted the sheets on his side. They were empty and cool, his heat already a distant memory.

A new pop rang out.

If that was a prelude to her neighbors playing their shitty music, she was going to reap them, consequences be damned. She struggled to her elbows, inhaled deeply at the effort and stilled at the bacon scent. Along with something else. She sniffed. *Cinnamon rolls? Smells like it.*

She shoved back her hair and pushed up.

Rafael was tending to two skillets on the stove and brandishing her spatula like a Food Network expert. Fried onion and potato scents wafted toward her.

His musk smelled better, scenting the sheets. He hadn't dressed. His glutes were rock hard and flexed with each move, his broad back potently male. Two creases ran down either side of his spine, nearly invisible, the only indication he had wings inside.

She ached to see, touch and explore them. For some reason, she found them sexy as hell.

But she shouldn't. They had no future. She had no right and couldn't figure out why he'd come back here after leaving. He must have taken off to get supplies, since she didn't have anything in the fridge except microwaveable crap. No fuss, no muss, no taste.

A fresh set of his clothes hung from her garment rack, the place being too small for a closet. His pants were navy, shirt pearl gray. He'd even brought another pair of stretchy boxer briefs and socks.

His feet were deliciously large with long toes. She'd never had a foot fetish before but with him she could develop one.

If good fortune was on her side, which it wasn't, she'd need years to explore him with her mouth, tongue and hands. He had too much badass stuff for her to enjoy. She wished he hadn't combed and tied back his hair. Loose was better. Tousled was staggering.

He opened the oven door and bent at the waist to peer inside. His cock swung back and forth, an erotic pendulum. Finished, he straightened, turned to her and smiled. Pleasure filled his eyes. They crinkled at the corners with his widening grin.

No one, ever, had greeted her like that. Usually lust filled their eyes then fear at what she really was.

Overcome by emotion, she left the bed and turned off the burners and oven.

He sobered. "What's wrong? You're not hungry?"

Starved was more like it. She wanted to laugh at her absurd feelings. Better that than cry. She sank to her knees and gripped his narrow hips. "Ravenous."

Some might say insatiable when it came to him. Unable to wait a second longer, she buried her face in his dark curls.

He pushed to his toes, swayed and sank back down.

She welcomed him with ardent attention, filled herself with his musk and ran her tongue down his thickening length. The velvety head was surprisingly salty, the prominent veins on his shaft masculine to the extreme. Both called to everything female within her, the same as his balls. Fleshy, pendulous, lightly furred.

Shamelessly, she eased his right ball into her mouth.

A grunt and growl rushed from him followed by incoherent words that were possibly angel-speak. He ended his noisy outburst with a crude oath.

Maybe he was a bad boy, after all.

She suppressed a smile and licked his nut good, loving its wrinkly texture rough with hair. Exactly the way a man should be. She tasted his other ball, as delicious as the first.

Something clanged on the stove. She guessed he'd tossed the spatula onto it.

He cupped her head in both hands, keeping her to him.

She never wanted to be anywhere else. If only wishes could come true. If only she could have been created as more than a damn reaper.

No such luck in her world.

Anguish tightened her chest. She pushed the horrible feeling aside and allowed unending desire to replace her grief. Pre-cum seeped from his erect rod and left a damp trail over her collarbone. It'd be an effort for her to take him fully inside her mouth, he was that long, but it would also be a labor of love. Half measures wouldn't do.

She cupped his tongue-dampened balls and eased his silky crown past her lips.

He cried out.

She responded with praise too soft for him to hear and opened her throat to guide his rod as deeply as it could go. He stopped wiggling and held his breath. Just as well. He'd lose it shortly.

With skill and tenderness, she guided him in farther and fondled his nuts.

He said something she didn't catch and dug his fingers into her scalp, anchoring him to her. Exactly where she wanted him to be.

For now. Later was another matter.

Pushing her misgivings aside, she concentrated on pleasure and took his shaft in inch by sensational inch. At last, her nose touched his fragrant curls.

He huffed. "Wow."

That wasn't remotely close to how ass-kicking great this was. Being close to him made existence a joy rather than a chore she had to slog through. These moments made her want. A dangerous notion. She pushed everything aside except her extreme carnal need and worked him in and out of her mouth, mirroring what her channel would do. Her tongue provided extra oomph by licking his length. Her lips sucked. A raw, passionate act and a moment celebrating exquisite affection. She'd never wanted anyone more.

He panted, tensed and fought his release but didn't endure as he had last night. His wild shout announced his climax.

She grasped his ass, held on with more desperation than she should have and accepted his cum greedily. The flavor was as unique as everything else about him — fresher than morning dew, richer than mousse, more satisfying than a cold drink on a steamy day.

Good God, I have to get a grip.

Reluctantly, she let him slip from her mouth. That didn't reduce her intense need. It battered her as nothing else had.

His firm belly quivered from his harsh breaths. He stroked her cheek. "That was epic. No, legendary. No...darn, I can't think of a better term. Thanks."

She wrapped her arms around his thighs.

He heaved in more air. "Want to eat? I'm cooking all your faves."

Of course he was. Everything about her was in her SACS file, right down to her culinary preferences. Reapers didn't need to eat, or sleep for that matter, but they could indulge if they wanted. A perk in an otherwise shitty job description. She'd always opted for those few mortal pastimes and he knew it. Her existence was an open book to him, making her even more powerless against his charm. She wanted to bitch at him for the unfairness in that but couldn't. His kind gesture moved her more than if he'd complimented her endlessly or given her diamonds and a lavish lifestyle. No one had ever made her breakfast, much less stuff she liked to eat. She hadn't a clue what he enjoyed. "I don't know anything about you."

That was beyond wrong.

"Don't worry. I'm a pretty fair cook."

She laughed softly at his sweet naiveté. "Not what I meant. First off, where'd the food come from?"

"Oh, I woke early and went to my place for clothes. Since you didn't have a lot here, I brought my stuff."

"Good angels eat?"

"They don't have to, but I like to indulge. Probably a residual pleasure from my time on Earth."

She hadn't expected that. After releasing him, she stood. "You were mortal?"

"Long, long time ago."

"This isn't cosmetic then?" She ran her forefinger around his navel.

He eased into her touch. "Nope. The real deal." He touched hers. "Yours?"

"An illusion." Like their relationship. Despair pressed close. She ignored it and swept her hand over her stomach. Her belly button disappeared, leaving smooth skin. "A few of my kind were born, like you. I was created." If that didn't prove the sorry truth about their incompatibility, nothing else would.

She padded away.

He caught her wrist before she got too far, reeled her back then turned on the burners and oven. "Tell me about your origins while I finish this."

"What's to tell? Everything about me is in my file."

"Not your earliest memories or what you failed to disclose in the personality tests." He wagged his finger. "Don't tell me you didn't fudge on those."

She'd lied through her teeth and had enjoyed doing so to give her then-PO a hard time. Rather than admit the truth or apologize, she shrugged. "You know me too well."

"I want to know you better. The real you. Tell me, please."

She couldn't. That would only deepen their bond, which was nuts. "Let me help." She checked the cinnamon rolls and flipped the potatoes.

Rafael didn't press, but he didn't pretend he'd forgotten either. He watched her play Suzy Homemaker, cooking up a storm. His silence began to annoy her and his patience touched her where few emotions could. She cracked. "Tell me about you first, then I'll share what I can about myself."

"Deal. While we eat." He filled their plates and brought them to the table.

"You take the chair." She pushed it to him. "I can sit on the bed."

"Like hell."

"Oh, yeah? Better watch it. You just said a four-letter word. My guess is it's your first. What's next? Expecting me to obey you? Not gonna happen. I refuse to take the chair."

"Too bad." He dropped into the seat, pulled her onto his lap and snuggled his arm around her waist. "What do you know, we both fit. It's a miracle." He sucked her neck.

His tongue tickled her. She giggled. "Like I said, you're a god."

"Wrong, I'm the man." He eased back. "At least a former one. Eat." He drew a bacon strip across her lips.

She gobbled it eagerly then sucked his fingers. "Fuck, that's good."

"There's more where that came from."

"I know. Let me lick your other fingers, your palms too, then your cock again. I'll smear bacon grease over it first."

"I was talking about food." He grabbed a cinnamon roll and fed her.

She allowed it. Stupid, of course, but she didn't want to stop. The sugary glaze and spice seduced her. He enthralled. "When were you mortal?"

He finished his bacon, a forkful of eggs and grabbed his orange juice. "Roman times."

"No shit. You were a Spartan like those guys in that flick *300*?"

He laughed, spitting up his OJ. "Sorry." He lapped drops from her nipples.

His tongue's warm, wet sweep registered in her DNA. Her head fell back. "Not a prob."

"Thanks." He kissed her throat. "Although I was born in Greece, I ended up as a Roman slave."

"Oh, no." Her stomach sank at the suffering he must have endured. She cupped his face. "Those pricks beat and starved you, didn't they?"

"Uh-uh, at least not the beating part. Food was definitely a problem though. When my master got in a snit, which happened frequently and for reasons unknown to me, he put me on starvation rations. Wasn't much I could do about it. As they say, beggars can't be choosers. Before I became a slave, I was a teacher by trade. I taught his kids math and stuff. It wasn't a bad gig, except for my mistress."

Unexpected jealousy reared its ugly head. She dismissed her feelings as ludicrous. They didn't go away. "Your master allowed you to have a girlfriend? That is, somebody's wife as a paramour? Wait." She dropped her hands. "You were married? Quit laughing at me." She slapped his arm.

His shoulders still shook. He flapped his hand in front of his face and finally calmed down. "By mistress, I meant lady of the house. When I finished teaching her boys for the day, I had to, uh…"

"What?"

He looked past, like he couldn't meet her gaze. "Tend to her needs."

Wynona hadn't seen that coming. "I'm guessing that doesn't mean showing her the ins and outs of equations."

His cheeks colored. "She wasn't very bright. She operated more on instinct and feelings rather than deep reasoning."

A nice way to say she was a nymph. "You slept with her?"

"Hey, not my choice. I didn't have much say in the matter. When she wanted a bath, a rubdown and some nookie, I had to perform."

"I'll bet. Did you enjoy it?" She got in his face. "Did. You. Come?"

"Are you jealous?"

She seethed with it when she shouldn't have. His illicit affair had happened a long time ago and had nothing to do with her. Yet, for him to be with anyone else wasn't something she could abide. She'd never had a significant other and didn't want to share him. Not even with someone who'd lived ages ago. "No."

His eyebrows lifted. "I'm glad. For a minute there, I thought you were going to rip out my tongue for confessing my past which amounted to doing as I was told."

"You didn't enjoy it—her then?"

He kissed her jawline. "If I hadn't been a slave, I would have taken off running."

"She was a real dog, huh?"

"Actually, she was quite lovely but not my type."

Wynona wanted to ask him what was but didn't have the nerve. She stroked his collarbone. "How'd you get anointed for sainthood and earn your wings with that past?"

"I'm no saint. I'm an angel."

"Same diff."

"Not hardly." He finished two cinnamon rolls before he focused on her. "As to how I got my wings...that's not something I like to talk about." Distress clouded his eyes.

She eased back his hair. "Why?"

"I'm ashamed."

She hugged him. "Why? Did you rat out your mistress to her husband and that saved your soul?"

"Uh-uh. My master and I didn't have regular chats, if you know what I mean. He barked orders, I hopped to it. No wasted words."

"You couldn't have done anything else wrong, like selling out a friend to get your wings. That's not like you. Please don't keep me hanging. I promise I won't judge. Hell, how could I? You know what I've done. None of it's good."

"That's not true." He pried her off him. Embarrassment flooded his face.

What he has to say must be mega bad. "Tell me. Maybe I can make things better."

He smiled wanly then sighed. "I saved my master and mistress' kids. That's how I got my wings."

That didn't make sense. "Did you have to kill them to rescue the kids? The parents were abusive and you told the authorities?"

"Not even close." He rested his fingertips on her mouth, quieting the other questions she had. "The kids were horsing around one afternoon at the Tiber. They both knew how to swim, but there'd been heavy flooding and the river roared through the city. Boys being boys, they decided to try their luck. I swam like a maniac to save the first one. Got him on shore and dove in for the second. He kept slipping away."

"Oh, my God." She covered her mouth. "The poor kid drowned?"

"No. Remember I said I saved them both?"

"Vaguely." She gripped his shoulders. "What happened?"

"I kept fighting the current. Wasn't anything else I could do. He was just a kid with so much to live for. He probably would have owned me after dear old dad kicked the bucket. Anyway, I finally got him, the second boy, on shore, too. Then there was the dog."

"What dog?"

"Their pet. He'd jumped in after them, planning his own rescue I suppose. I tried like hell to pull him to shore but by then I was exhausted and couldn't fight any longer. Poor thing drowned. I'll never forgive myself for that."

He was definitely too good if that was what caused his shame...unless something else had. "What happened when you couldn't save him?" She frowned. "Please don't tell me those pricks beat you because you didn't rescue their mutt and you fought back in self-defense and that's why you feel bad."

"Nope. I never touched them. I drowned with the dog. They found my body downstream a week later."

Her mouth trembled. "You *died*?"

"Well, yeah. I would have eventually, anyway. That was a long time ago. Hey, there's no reason to cry."

She couldn't stop.

"At least I got my wings for what I considered a pretty sloppy rescue."

She slipped off his lap. "Stand up."

"Why?"

"Just. Do. It."

"Okay, okay. Stop bouncing." He pushed to his feet. "We gonna hug?"

She slapped his hands from her and circled him.

He turned. "What are you looking for?"

Hickeys, scratches, love bites or other evidence of their time together. She couldn't recall if she'd marked him during their lust-crazed session last night. "Quit turning around and following me. Stand still."

"Take it easy."

She couldn't. Too much was at stake. "What's your plan when your boss or SACS asks where you were last night?"

"No one will."

"You're sure of that. Let's pretend you're wrong. Since you can't lie, what exactly did you intend to tell them if they ask?"

"They won't. They trust me."

"They shouldn't."

He sagged. "You don't mean that. You can't. Please stop crying."

"I'm not."

He wiped a tear from her cheek and licked it off his finger.

She sagged into him. "I don't want you to get caught. You'll ruin your career and your future and for what, this?" She gestured to her crappy place. Even a homeless person would have found it wanting unless he or she was into BDSM.

"No. This." He brushed his mouth over hers.

A sob bubbled up. She shoved it back down. "Show me your wings."

He ground his cock against her cleft. "They really turn you on, huh?"

"No. Yes. Dammit, stop it." She broke away and clenched her fists. "I need to see if I broke them last night."

"Are you kidding? Granted, you're a tigress in bed, but you're not that wild. Besides, if you had hurt them, I would have screeched like a little girl."

She clenched her teeth. "Show. Me."

He threw up his hands, turned his back to her and let loose.

The unfurling was strikingly sexy, his right wing grazing the table. A fork fell off and clattered on the floor. He looked over.

Wynona gasped at the black marks smudging his once-pristine wings. "Oh, my God, oh, my God, oh, my freaking God."

"What?"

He struggled to look behind himself and turned so fast, his wing swept potatoes off his plate and knocked a cinnamon roll onto the chair. He spun in the other direction. That wing whizzed toward the skillets.

She grabbed his shoulders. "Don't move." Her head fell forward. "This can't be happening."

"*What?* Tell me."

"Stay here. Close your eyes."

"Why?"

"Do it. Please."

She ran into the bath, dampened a washcloth and prayed she hadn't seen what she had. Maybe when he'd ascended to Heaven for his duds and the food, he'd brushed up against something dirty without recalling it. She shot back into the room. Her hopes crumbled. There was more darkness on his wings than she'd realized. Her belly hurt so badly she doubled over from the pain and gasped.

Rafael's lids snapped open. He took one look at her and turned white. "What's wrong?"

"Don't move." Fighting pain and panic, she dragged the chair over, stood on it and ran the cloth over his right wing.

He trembled.

"I said don't move."

"I can't help it. That feels good."

It wouldn't when he saw what she did. Each wing was way worse than she'd thought, fully black at the top, the color diminishing to gray an eighth of the way down. Even so, it had to be dirt, mud or maybe even tar, the only things that made sense. Holding back a whimper, she brushed as lightly as she could. The stain didn't budge. She rubbed harder.

He lurched away. "Hey, stop. That hurts."

Her legs gave out. She sank to the chair and held out the cloth to him.

He glanced at it. "What am I supposed to be looking for?"

"Dirt, mud, grease, tar or something else — take your pick."

"I don't see anything."

"I know. It won't come off your wings."

"What won't?" He looked over and stilled.

Now he got it. "Wait. Maybe I need to use soap or shampoo." She jumped to her feet and pulled him into the bath.

Rafael hoped to God Wynona's plan worked. Not so much for his sake, for hers.

She dropped the soap twice, cursed the bar, kicked the tub and grabbed the shampoo. Her grip was too tight, her aim damn bad. A stream of the strawberry-scented stuff hit his chin, neck and pecs.

She groaned. "Sorry."

"S'okay. It'll wash off."

"On your chest, but what if the black doesn't come off your wings?" She bounced on her heels. "What if you're ruined?"

He should have cared but didn't. Spending last night with her had been the only true happiness he'd ever known. As a man, he'd died before experiencing real love. As a good angel, he'd dedicated himself to Heaven's cause and considered his lingering carnal desires a failing. Something he'd eventually get over.

After the few nights he'd spent with Ursula, he'd been ready to embrace celibacy. Then Wynona had stomped into his life, a bundle of contradictions and sass wrapped in pure female allure.

He smiled. No, he glowed.

She scraped shampoo off his chest, worked up lather and applied the bubbles to the top feathers on his left wing. His lids slipped down. Blindly, he reached for the sink and grabbed the edge for support before his legs folded.

She jerked back. "Did I hurt you again?"

He was about to come. There were as many nerve endings in his feathers as his rod. Pleasure stormed between his legs and centered in his balls. "Feels good."

"You sound like you're in pain."

Only because his shaft wasn't burrowed within her. Them being apart hurt him worse than any physical injury could. Her worry pained him deeply. "I'm fine. Please relax."

"Soon as your wings are back to normal."

"They'll be fine."

"Hold still." She scooped water from the basin, poured it over the lather and moaned. "It's not working."

"Let's take a shower."

"What? No. Maybe toothpaste will do the trick. It has grit to scour junk off teeth. I have a whitening brand." She whooped. "That should work great with my electric toothbrush."

He caught her wrist before she could grab the thing and scour his plumage.

She patted his arm with her free hand. "I swear I'll be careful. If this doesn't work, I can get peroxide or hair dye from the drugstore and bleach you back to the way you should be. Why didn't I think of that before? I should try it first. It'll be quicker."

He pulled her into him. "Don't go."

"I'll only be gone for a few minutes."

"Too long." He brushed his lips over hers and slipped his tongue inside.

She slumped against him, her mouth loose and willing beneath his.

He tasted her tears, worry, sorrow and what he knew was her deepening bond with him. No one had ever fallen apart on his behalf as she had. He'd been an orphan in Greece, his indifferent uncle raising him. He suspected the man hadn't worried a moment about his capture and subsequent slavery. His Roman master had been equally callous, paying little attention to him unless he didn't obey quickly enough or needed more to eat than the usual starvation rations. His celestial bosses were kind, but their love wasn't unconditional. They weren't family.

Wynona could be. She wanted him in spite of who he was. She cared about his future when she didn't give a crap about her own. He had to change things for her and them. How, he had no idea. Maybe he'd get an idea once they both relaxed.

He tore his mouth free and pulled her to the tub. "How about that shower? The mist might make the black go away faster. You can scrub me all you want while I scrub you."

She lowered her face. "You can't get rid of my darkness. It runs too deep."

"You're too hard on yourself."

She tilted her head and looked at him. "Aren't you the one who's been bitching about my mishaps?"

"That's not the real you. Come on." He helped her into the tub, folded his wings, got in too and closed the shower curtain on them. The lavender plastic made the small space wonderfully colorful and cozy. "While I wash you, I want to hear about your earliest memories and what you didn't admit to in the personality tests."

She wrapped her arms around herself. "Sounds more like an interrogation than a shower."

He held her chin between his thumb and forefinger. "Trust me. I'll go easy on you."

She glanced at his cock, so rigid it defied gravity and pointed at her cunt. "Uh-huh."

With warm water misting around them and his soapy hands on her boobs, he backed her into the wall. "Relax."

"I don't think I can with you thumbing my nipples."

"I can always stop."

"And risk getting one of my knees to your balls for depriving me?"

He fondled her gently. A flush spread across her cheeks. He adored his effect on her. More importantly, her happiness made his existence worthwhile. "How far back do you remember? How old were you then?"

She lifted her face to the ceiling. Her lids slid down. "I'd just been created. One minute I had no conscious thought and in the next there I was, all grown up, looking exactly as you see me now, totally nude, and eye to eye with TGR."

"Who's that?"

"The Grim Reaper. Death. Call him whatever you will, it's the same concept. I asked him who he was. Wait. I asked him who I was. I recall him laughing. '*Not who, what,*' he said. '*Reapers like you aren't people. You were never mortal. You're not anything.*'"

Rafael couldn't believe anyone or anything could be such an SOB. TGR's callousness must have been devastating for a newly created being. What he'd said to Wynona was all she knew of the world. He could have given her some hope to make her burden easier. "I'm so sorry."

She swallowed hard but waved dismissively. "I didn't know any better at the time, so it was no big deal. I told myself he was just a mean old turd or seriously deluded about my state. I actually believed that until I reaped my first soul, no more than an hour after he created me." She shrugged. "At least I had sixty minutes to build myself up into something I wasn't."

He hugged her as hard as he dared, not wanting to hurt her further. "You shouldn't have had to go through what you did."

"No kidding. Imagine if I hadn't been created as a reaper. I wouldn't have made your existence such hell these last days."

"I didn't mean that."

"I know." She eased away and smiled sadly. "Although I'm hardcore about my reaping, the kids and teens have always been the worst. For the longest time, I kept asking him why I couldn't swap someone else's soul for theirs. The world's never had a shortage of psychopaths. Who'd miss one? Same with crooked politicians, maniacs who start wars, control freaks who beat up women so they'll feel like men, or jerks who make everyone's life miserable. Rather than listen to my pleas, he always told me to shut up then said the same thing—I couldn't reap them because it wasn't their time. Yeah, yeah, yeah. Who wrote that stupid rule?"

Rafael eased her hair over her shoulder.

Her eyes glistened. "Eventually, I just went through the motions, then the nineteen-fifties rolled around." She shook her head. "I'm too embarrassed to tell you any more."

"I won't laugh or judge. You didn't with me."

"That's because you're a good guy. After you hear what I have to say, you'll think I'm nuts."

He cradled her cheek. "Never. Please go on."

"I shouldn't."

"Please."

She clutched her throat and averted her gaze. "When I saw how the kids in this country were having fun during the fifties, I wanted to go to high school, too, and be a teenybopper. I dreamt of frilly prom dresses, dating the football captain, attending college, having a life with the white picket fence, two kids and a dog. Stupid stuff."

"Not stupid. Sweet."

"You feel sorry for me."

He loved her. Completely. Mindlessly. Her file picture had captivated him first. She'd smirked at the camera as gangsters did in their mug shots. Reading about her many escapades had intrigued him. Meeting her had stolen his breath. He'd fought his feelings, striving for indifference. It hadn't worked.

No way could he tell her how he felt. She wasn't ready. He hoped someday she would be.

"No, never sorry." He stroked her cheek. "I admire you for surviving an impossible existence that you didn't choose. When I died, Frank at least gave me a choice."

"Frank?"

"My CO, commanding officer, boss, you know. He said I could serve Heaven for eternity or close my eyes and that'd be it. No more pain."

"Why didn't you close your eyes to avoid additional shit?"

"There wouldn't have been any pleasure, either." He wouldn't have met her. It had taken him long enough, but the miracle had happened. "I don't know if I could have managed to do what you have. I'm not that good a man. I'm not that brave."

"Hush." She rested her forehead against his. "You're a god."

"I'm glad you think so."

"Not think. Know." She kissed him deep and long.

He coaxed her into his arms, her legs around his hips, and mounted her standing up, driving his cock into her cunt effortlessly. No surprise. They'd been created for each other. The fact that she didn't have a navel, parents, had never experienced childhood or any mortal stuff didn't make him want to run away. It pissed him off, saddened him too.

Her being a reaper made him love her even more, if that were possible.

She did the world's dirty work and everyone reviled her for it. She was stronger than any man he'd met, better than every good angel he knew. One act of kindness or bravery had given them a ticket to Heaven. She'd fought for children's lives, wanted to right wrongs, needed to haul the bad guys in.

For that, the powers that be had branded her a rebel. Screw them.

He pumped into her, not savagely as he had last night, but with tenderness and respect. She was his woman now. Hopefully, she'd go along with the plan.

They kissed until they needed air, bellowed their respective climaxes, laughed and stumbled to bed. Relaxed for the first time in forever, Rafael couldn't wait to sleep. He reached for her.

She backed into her nightstand, bumping the lamp. Amber-colored light streamed across the mattress. Her face went slack.

Rafael looked over. The formerly gray parts on his wings were now black, the discoloration taking up even more on each wing. "It's all right."

"The hell it is." She tugged on a lacy red thong.

"What are you doing?"

"Getting dressed." She threw on a short leather skirt, long leather top and boots that reached her thighs, each item in black. "I'm getting the peroxide and hair dye. Be right back."

During her absence, he smelled the sheets and her clothing, worshipping her scent. He planned their future and prayed she'd go along with his ideas. As far as living arrangements were concerned, they'd be roomies here. Each day, she'd go to work at From Crud to Stud and he'd follow to keep her in line with his hands, mouth, tongue and cock.

He was on the verge of masturbating to his X-rated fantasies when she returned, her arms cradling bags.

"In the bath, pronto." She used every product she'd bought at the same time.

They burned like mad, but he tried not to wince.

Wynona raced back and forth, blowing on his wings to ease the pain. When he was finally comfortable, she held his hand. "Everything's going to be all right. This will work."

The timer dinged. She shoved him into the shower and turned on the water full blast. He gagged at the awful chemical odors.

She checked his feathers, sank to the floor and buried her face in her hands.

Chapter Seven

That night, Wynona arrived at the service early, which she'd never done. Living on the edge and pissing people off had been her only goal.

Not any longer.

She hurried inside.

Heather had her face raised to the flickering lights. She turned, saw Wynona and flinched. "Oh, didn't know it was you. I should have guessed because of the... I shouldn't have said that. I didn't mean anything bad. I'm sorry. Can you forgive —"

"No prob." Wynona could barely keep still. "Is MJ here, too?"

Heather pushed back in her chair. "Why?"

Good Lord, she wasn't going to reap MJ's soul, since the genie didn't have one, nor was Wynona interested in her as a potential lover. "I need to talk to her."

"Oh." She pointed her pen to the left. "MJ's in her office."

The genie had her feet propped on the desk, hands behind her head. *Sons of Anarchy* played on her computer screen. She didn't bother looking up. "Please don't tell me I have a client already. Jax's about to kick some ass. For a mortal, he's wicked hot."

"We need to talk." Wynona closed the door and shut the laptop, cutting off the program.

MJ made a face. "I know you're still pissed at us for supposedly hurting your feelings. But, just so you know, you're living dangerously here."

"Seriously? What can little old you do to mean old me? I'm a freaking reaper. Death has already screwed me big time. In the scheme of things, you're a gnat."

"Wow, you have a nice way of starting a conversation after giving me the silent treatment for weeks." She brought her feet down.

Her bells tinkled.

The buttons on her crimson silk blouse were open to her bra, her jeans tighter than the skinny ones once in vogue. Downright modest for MJ, considering she liked to show up in little more than chains that barely hid her nudity. The clients hadn't complained.

Wynona leaned in. "I need a wish." MJ granted them to customers, for a price, as an extra part of the service. "I'm willing to pay whatever you want. Money's no object."

"Must be some wish."

It was more important than her fifties fantasy. "You gotta do this now."

"Back up a little. If you're intending to wish me, Becca, Heather and Constance out of existence, I can't oblige. Sorry."

"That's not what I want. You're all safe from me."

"All righty then. I can give you the employee discount." MJ pulled out her wish form. "That should ease the pain a bit. Fill this out."

Wynona slid the sheet right back. "No form. No record. This has to be a secret between us."

MJ's violet eyes glittered. "I'm all ears. You want to be mortal now? Or a guy maybe? An animal?"

"No...could you actually make me mortal?"

"Nope. Just wondering."

Wynona wanted to smack her. "The wish isn't for you to do something to me, but to Rafael."

"Oh, hey." MJ held up her hands. "I don't off good angels."

"I don't want you to kill him, which isn't possible anyway. I want you to fix him."

"I don't do vasectomies, either."

Wynona held back a scream. "I'm not worried about his balls. His feathers have turned black. Not all of them, just the top half. They should be white as the driven snow. Not off-white, not ecru, but white-white, the kind that makes you squint and will burn out your irises if you don't wear shades. You know, exactly like the clothes Heather always wears. I want to wish his wings back to the way they were and keep them that way forever."

"Technically, that's two wishes."

Another second of this and she'd strangle MJ. "Fine. I'll pay whatever you want. Just get it done pronto."

"There are a few formalities first." She rummaged in her desk and slid another paper over. "Have him fill this out, in triplicate, initial each page and sign at the bottom."

Wynona tore up the form and tossed the pieces in the wastebasket. "He can't know how this happened. It just has to."

"In that case, no can do."

"Why the hell not?"

"Third-party wishes aren't allowed without the receiving party's consent. If they were, anyone could wish any horrible thing on someone else without their knowledge or consent."

"I don't want him hurt. I want him back the way he was, not the way he is now."

"Did he bruise his feathers? Maybe the black will go away."

"It's freaking permanent. If several bottles of peroxide and L'Oréal's extreme platinum mixed together can't lighten it, nothing will."

MJ folded her arms on the desk and leaned forward. "You saw his wings? You dyed them? What happened between you guys?" She grinned slyly. "Things got a little rough while you did the deed?"

Wynona was close to tears. "Please, you have to help me."

"I wish I could." MJ actually looked sympathetic. "But I can't make a move unless he agrees."

His damn stupid integrity wouldn't let him. That morning, when the chemicals had failed, he'd been stoic rather than concerned, telling her it was for the best. He couldn't deliberately con Frank and SACS. Wouldn't be right. He'd rather suffer the consequences than lie. *What a freaking fool.*

No matter how she'd shouted, pleaded or cried, he wouldn't budge. If his wings turned black and fell off because they made love, so be it. He was ready to dive in for more, wanting them to screw in the shower again, on the table, floor, bed, every-goddamned-where, no matter the consequences.

Men. Always thinking with their little head rather than their big one.

She raced from MJ's office to Becca's and slammed the door, closing them inside.

Becca jerked and looked over from her laptop. She was watching *The Blacklist. Doesn't anyone work here?* "We need to talk."

Surprise swept her features. She turned off the video. "Of course. Sit down. I'm so glad we're having a chance to iron out what happened."

"I'm still pissed about that. Maybe next week I'll feel different." Wynona pointed at Becca's smartphone. "Call your mom."

"Why?" She looked at her office phone. "Did Heather tell you to tell me to phone my mother? Isn't Heather's intercom working?"

"I don't know." Wynona planted her hands on Becca's desk. "I need a potion or spell or both from your mom."

"What—why?"

"Because I can't count on yours to turn out right the first time. Maybe the second time, either."

Becca crossed her arms. "You have a funny way of breaking the ice between us and asking for a favor."

"Sorry. I don't have time for pleasantries. Please, call your mom for me. I'd do it myself but I don't have her number."

"She's unlisted. What kind of spell or potion did you want?"

"I don't know. I'm not a witch."

"What did you want the magic to do?"

"Swear you won't tell anyone, especially Rafael."

"You're not trying to off him, are you?"

What is with these people? "No, I'm trying to help him." She explained the problem, pacing as she did. By the time she'd finished, she was winded and sagged against the wall. "Surely, there has to be a potion or spell that can help."

"Only if he agrees to it."

"*Why?*" She stomped across the room, hands flapping. "And don't give me that third-party shit. Witches cast spells on poor schmucks all the time, doing all sorts of crappy things to them."

"That's second-party, not third. And only bad witches do that, not good ones like me and my mom."

"Finally, we're getting somewhere. Do you have a list of the bad ones? Their phone numbers? Websites? Email addies? Something?"

"We don't associate with them. Can't you just talk to him?"

Wynona shook so badly from frustration, her teeth rattled. "I did until my voice went out. He won't listen. He's laser-focused on us fooling around."

"Maybe you shouldn't."

Now, she got that advice. Pissing little good it did her. "I've already told him no way are we ever, and I do mean ever, getting together again, not even if I'm able to fix this. I don't want him hurt. I couldn't bear doing anything bad to him." Tears slipped down her cheeks.

"Oh, my God, you poor baby." Becca came around her desk and hugged her. "This isn't your fault. You didn't know."

"He asked me to corrupt him and I did." She rested her chin on Becca's shoulder. "I should be shot. I wish I could be."

"Shhh. You don't mean that. Maybe he'll come around and agree to magic."

Not in a zillion years. He was too honest and possibly a masochist, too, given the shit he was willing to face. "I have to do something." She pulled away and ran to the door.

"Where are you going?"

"I don't know." A bold-faced lie, but she didn't have time to get into the truth. She ran into Constance's office.

Huddled close to her laptop, she spoke baby talk to Gabe, her mortal boyfriend and a New Orleans cop. Two qualities that should have kept them apart, considering Constance was a voodoo priestess and worked in this nut house. Somehow, the world hadn't ended when Gabe had found out about her and everyone else here. He was too much in love and kept the secret.

He probably wouldn't have felt the same if Constance had been a reaper.

Wynona slammed the door.

Constance slid her gaze over then focused on the screen. "Can I call you back, sweetie? One of the staff just tried to break my door."

"Are you all right, babe? Want me to come over?"

She leveled her gaze at Wynona. "No, I can handle this." After blowing him a kiss, she killed the call and squinted. "Are you crying?"

"No." She swiped tears from her cheeks. "I'm allergic."

"To this place?" Constance arched one eyebrow. "If you're here to rag on me, I'm not apologizing to you again for something I didn't do. You need to lose the attitude, lady."

At any other time, Wynona would have threatened the apocalypse. She forced herself to be sweet and submissive, two behaviors she loathed, unless it was during BDSM play with a Dom. "I need your help...your special help."

Constance leaned forward. "You want me to remove your memories of this place?"

"No." She backed away. As much as she hated to admit it, she'd grown used to coming here, scaring the shit out of weres and intimidating vamps or reapers. She'd especially enjoyed how Becca and the others had groveled these last weeks, trying to get back in her good graces.

She did have a shitty attitude and would try to work on it as soon as she settled this. "I want you to remove Rafael's memories of me."

Maybe if he forgot her, everything could return to normal for him.

Constance tapped a tapered nail against her cheek. "He's giving you a hard time, huh?"

She has no idea. "This is personal, not work related. I'll still do my time here. He just won't remember who I am."

"Okay, you lost me. How could that work?"

He wouldn't be her PO any longer. Once he forgot who she was, he'd panic, return to Heaven and they'd send Xavier or someone else down, chalking up Rafael's memory loss and blackened wings to toxic air, water or her driving him nuts. After a long rest, he might be able to move on to another case.

The plan wasn't perfect, but it was the only one she had. "I'll pay you whatever you want. Twice the going rate. Hell, fifty times. Name your price."

"No can do."

She growled. "Doesn't anyone here say yes to anything?"

"Hey, I would if I could. I can see you're hurting." She regarded Wynona. "Why? What happened between you two?"

"What didn't?"

"Oh, yeah?" Constance left her chair, her mint-green gown fluttering around her curves. "We are talking about the same thing, right? The eagle has landed. You two did the nasty. You got down and—"

"What we did was beyond anything you could imagine."

"I doubt that." She pressed her hand to her throat. "Was it good for you?"

"Try paradise on steroids."

"Little wonder. He's a definite hottie."

"You have no idea. His wingspan alone..." She shivered.

Constance pulled her to the sofa. "Sit. I want to hear every gory detail."

"I'll give you all the particulars if you promise to remove his memories of me without his consent or his knowledge that you're going to do so. Nothing in writing, either."

"That would be unethical."

"That's too bad." Wynona stood. "My lips are sealed."

"I could always ask him."

"But you won't, because you're my friend. Please say you are. I mean it." Wynona needed Constance, Becca and the others. She'd never felt more alone.

"You bet." Constance patted her hand. "Wish I could help on the other stuff, too."

"So do I." She hurried from the room and ran to the reception area.

Heather froze in her chair, her grin painfully stiff. "Hi."

"Yeah. We're friends, right?"

"Oh, I hope so." She sighed and relaxed, color returning to her cheeks. "These last weeks have been terrible. It's awful when anyone's angry with me. I'm so glad you're not any longer."

Wynona stepped toward the hall. "Has Rafael come in yet?"

"A few minutes ago. He asked for you. I told him you were talking to MJ."

Crap, she didn't need that. "Is he with her now?" Listening to what she said about performing wishes on him without his consent?

"No. The break room. Want me to get him for you?"

Wynona grabbed Heather's wrist before she could skip away. "Nope. But I do have a favor. As my friend, you'll help, right?"

She sat. "I'll do the best I can."

"That's not good enough, sweetie." She hated to play with Heather's head, but now wasn't the time to be fair or kind. "Friends don't qualify favors. They do them. They succeed."

Heather nodded so quickly her hair bounced. "I will. I hope." She bit her bottom lip.

Nothing was going right today. Wynona leaned in to avoid anyone overhearing them. "This isn't hard, really. I'd like you to heal Rafael."

"He's sick?"

If she meant in the head, then only a resounding yes would do. Wynona was as wacky for wanting him. She explained the situation again and smiled non-threateningly. "So you can help?"

Heather pulled in her shoulders.

She wanted to die. Too bad that wasn't an option. "Let me guess. Unless he wants you to heal his wings, it's no can do."

"I'm so sorry. I'll try to heal whatever's wrong with them, if he lets me. But if he doesn't, I can't trick him, lie, cheat or anything like that to get it done. That would be wrong. Forgive me for saying so, but I can't—"

"Right. Tell you what, forget the healing for now. Talk to him as one perfect person to the other. Both of you are pure goodness and all that other stuff. He'll listen to you."

"About what?"

"Tell him he needs to get his wings fixed. Explain his very existence depends upon doing so, because it does. He can do it with your healing, a wish from MJ or a potion and spell from Becca's mom. As a backup, he can have Constance remove his memories of me. Tell me you can convey that to him and convince him of it."

Her complexion was pasty again. "Why would he want to forget you?"

"I'm poison to him. You have to make him see the truth."

"Oh, no. I can't believe it. You're a good person."

Typical Heather, totally sweet and completely oblivious. "This one time, I'm trying to be. I'm counting on your help."

She squared her shoulders. "Okay. I'll do it."

"You'll succeed."

She wilted. "Be right back."

"No, take your time. The rest of the night if you need it. I'll watch the front desk. Manage things for you."

"Promise you'll be good? I hate to ask. It's awful that I did, but—"

"I won't mess up anything, I swear." She gave her the Boy Scout salute.

Heather dragged away to do her duty.

Wynona wrung her hands and paced, stopping at a white flash in the hall. Heather crossed from the break room into a treatment area, Rafael following her. Before he could glance her way, Wynona ducked behind the wall and held her breath.

A door closed gently.

She haunted the empty hall and waited. The first seconds were excruciating, the next torture. She paced worse than a caged animal. This was like waiting for a jury's verdict of life in prison without parole or death, neither being the ideal sentence.

Never seeing Rafael again would tear her apart, but bringing him down would destroy her. She couldn't live with the anguish. She'd want that special place in Hell then, all the misery Satan and his minions could heap on her.

The front door opened. A cool breeze slid inside.

Olaf slipped in and glared. "I want to talk to your boss."

"Join the club. She's in the West Indies, some kind of witch convention. How can I help you?"

"Haven't you done enough already?"

He was still pissed about what happened at the Crucible. "I shouldn't have taken off last night like I did. My bad. But the guy I was with was an old friend." She tried an apologetic smile. "Forgive me?"

"Where are we going tonight?"

She wanted to ask if that would be after she threw him through the wall or once she'd hurled, but kept her cool. "I have plans."

"Me too. I want to see the next in command."

"She's in Haiti. Some kind of voodoo thing."

"Hey there." Becca strolled into the reception area. "Welcome to From Crud to Stud."

He took in her harem getup, tonight's ensemble in teal. "Who are you?"

"No one." Wynona shot Becca a please-don't-say-anything look and ushered Olaf to the door. "Come back when everyone's here." She shoved him out and turned to Becca. "I'll explain later."

"Uh-huh."

Heather left the treatment room and slogged down the hall when she should have been skipping and singing a Disney tune.

What she had to report couldn't be good. Wynona backed up. Her ass hit the door.

The knob turned and rattled. "Let me in." Olaf banged on the door.

She pressed against it.

Heather stopped and lowered her face, shoulders sagging. "I tried. I really did. He said no way, ever, for any healing or magic."

Rafael lay facedown on a treatment table, arms hanging over the sides. Daemon patted his head. Taro and Anatol slouched against the wall and watched him closely, their downturned mouths pitying him.

Stefin yawned then stretched. His sulfur stench intensified. "Why are we in here?"

Anatol rolled his eyes. "Wynona dumped Rafael."

"Hey, congratulations." Stefin smacked Rafael's shoulder. "Where are we celebrating? Not the Crucible. Let's try someplace new. Anyone up for the second circle of Hell tonight?"

Taro mouthed, "*Moron.*"

Rafael rolled his forehead over the padded leather. After Wynona's chemicals had failed, she'd refused to corrupt him further even though constant sex was his obvious choice. He couldn't go back to being a perfect angel any more than ex-virgins could reclaim their purity. So why not enjoy themselves? He'd told her that, too.

She'd thrown him out of her apartment. He'd walked the city for hours, afraid to unfurl his wings and ascend to Heaven. Once there, Frank and the others might take him into custody, never letting him see her again.

That would be the real hell.

When he'd come in tonight, he'd hoped she'd softened somewhat, missing him as much as he had her. By the time he'd asked if she'd arrived, he was hyperventilating, his palms sweaty. When Heather had come into the break room, he'd nearly cheered. He'd thought Wynona had sent for him, not made more plans to get him out of her life and her out of his head, eager to have Constance obliterate those precious memories.

He muttered obscenities as he'd never done before.

"Still hurts, huh?" Daemon kneaded his back.

Knife-sharp pain shot down Rafael's shoulders and arms, stealing his breath. Not only were his muscles sore, his feathers were nearly raw from the dyes. "Thanks, but I'm good."

"That's your problem." Stefin wagged his finger. "You put up with Wynona's crap for too long."

Taro snorted. "Just like you still do with Zoe's. The same as us."

"Hey." Anatol pushed away from the wall and held up his hands. "That's the answer to this problem." He spoke to Rafael. "Remember what we said about Zoe pulling the same stuff on us in the beginning and telling us to leave her alone?"

Stefin laughed. "We gave her exactly what she wanted. My idea, by the way, to use reverse psychology. Don't forget it or that term."

"I'm not playing games with Wynona." He frowned. "I am not giving up on her, either." She was his woman.

"Of course, you're not letting her go." Anatol pulled his dreadlocks into a ponytail. "But she won't know that. You'll be polite and emotionally distant, as though she means nothing to you. You'll also happen to be wherever she is, bumping into her lightly, brushing against her, standing close until she caves and jumps you. Get the idea?"

Sounds juvenile but strangely sexy. "Why can't she and I simply talk this out?"

They laughed.

Rafael rolled off the table, catching himself before he fell.

Stefin blocked the door. "You better listen to us. This is the only way to turn a woman around. If you crowd her, she'll run. Give her what she thinks she wants and she'll be in your arms in no time at all."

Or she'll forget me and return to the Crucible with Olaf. "Are you sure this will work? I'm dying here."

Taro crossed his arms. "How's your plan working?"

Outside of shittily, he'd have to say pissing bad. "Guess I'll give this a try."

"Good man." Stefin shoved Rafael into the hall. "Do us proud."

As if he'd want to go that far. However, begging Wynona for a hug was probably out of the question.

Rafael smoothed his clothes and strode into the treatment room on wobbly legs, so short of breath he was barely conscious.

Wynona looked over. Her cheeks colored.

His entire being ached for her, but he played Mr. Professional and focused on the zombie strapped to the treatment table, an ugly dude with vacant gray eyes. "Is this your first time restraining a customer?"

"No. Of course not."

"Just asking. I wasn't being critical." He joined her, standing so close their arms touched. She tensed but didn't move away. He couldn't have asked for better. "First zombie for you?"

"No."

She sounded as breathless as he did.

"Do you mind if I make a suggestion?"

She cleared her throat. "I don't know. What?"

"Loosen the strap on his wrist."

When Rafael had come in, she'd tugged the restraint so hard the zombie's hand had broken off and hung by a tendon now. That wouldn't last long. Tissue stretched and snapped. The hand plopped on the floor.

Wynona reached for the thing. Rafael did, too. Their fingertips touched. A lightning bolt from God couldn't have registered deeper in his psyche. He backed away first and placed the appendage between the guy's legs.

She pointed. "I didn't do that deliberately."

"I'll put that in my report."

"You're writing me up?" She poked his chest. "Is this because I asked Heather to talk to you?"

"No. It's because I'm your PO." He pivoted. "For the moment."

"Hold it." She joined him. "Someone else is taking over my case?" Relief and sadness played across her beautiful features.

An urge to hug her hit him harder than an eighteen-wheeler. Recalling Stefin's advice, he forced himself to shrug like Mr. Cool would. "I won't be here forever. I'd like to write a good report on you for the next person." That wasn't a lie. If she really wanted him gone, he'd have no choice except to leave her be. "Tell your new PO what a great job you're doing."

The zombie held up his stump and grunted.

Wynona rushed to the doorway. "Heather!"

Rafael patted the guy's knee. "Heather's the healer here. She'll fix you up in a jiff."

She rushed inside, her pale hair and white skirt flying. "Oh, my."

Wynona backed away from her and toward him.

Unwillingly, Rafael put distance between them, playing the indifferent bastard. "I'll observe from over here. Just pretend I'm not around, like I've already moved on."

He stood near the wall, insides shaking, but his determination remained firm. He had to win her over no matter what.

Chapter Eight

During her shift, Wynona became increasingly dangerous to clients. Not by choice, however. She couldn't concentrate. Without thinking, she grabbed a were's arm to escort him to the treatment room. He gasped and dropped to the floor.

Heather restarted his heart. Becca gave him a fifty percent discount on that night's services.

Things didn't go any better with a vamp. During his aversion therapy, which used electric shocks, Wynona hurried into his room to get restraints. A definite no-no. The lights flickered immediately. By the time she realized her error, the electricity spiked, sending a mega jolt through him.

Daemon had to pry the vamp off the ceiling.

Becca wrote off his treatment charge and gave him a coupon for the following week's session. Rather than bitching, she stroked Wynona's arm. "Maybe you should take the rest of the night off and relax."

Wouldn't do any good. She'd toss in bed, missing Rafael's embrace, him filling her. Tomorrow would be more of the same. He'd watch quietly, his presence arousing and unnerving. Or he'd be gone, leaving her with nothing but sweet-painful memories. Either way, she was screwed and had to tough this out.

While Becca consoled her, footfalls sounded. Rafael was in the hall and met Wynona's gaze. Desire surged through her and burrowed deep, along with raw despair. She wasn't certain which was worse—how horribly distant he'd become or how he waited patiently, without comment or complaint, for her to screw up again. With her performance tonight, she'd probably end up with Attila the Hun as her next PO.

She sagged. "I'm not doing this on purpose, I swear."

Becca patted her arm. "I know. How about you stick with reapers for the remainder of your shift?"

Sounded like a plan. She couldn't do much harm to her own kind.

Before the next hour was out, her reaper client had backed into a corner and shook like a beaten dog. "It's not working. You need to stop."

She'd talked him into bleaching his feathers, telling him mortal babes liked white wings better than black ones. Her hope had been that the ingredients for Becca's potions would do the trick, which Wynona would then use on Rafael's wings. No dice. The reaper's feathers littered the floor, a good portion of his wings bald now.

Rafael stood to the side, amazingly quiet considering this newest fiasco.

She was ready to burst and whirled on him. His impassive demeanor spiked her frustration. "I didn't do that on purpose."

"I know."

She held back a sob. "I did this for you."

The reaper whimpered. "What kind of service is this? He wanted you to torture me?"

"Of course not." She turned back to Rafael. "You need to fix yourself."

"What about me?" The reaper touched a bare spot on his wing and moaned.

Wynona fled the room and ran down the hall.

Heather looked up from her computer screen. "You need me to heal someone or something again?"

"Reaper, room nine. I'm leaving for the night. Tell Becca, please."

Wynona rushed outside and gulped the cool, humid air. A dog howled. Others followed, their racket quickly annoying. Wind gusted. Lights flickered. She raced away from the building, past locals and tourists talking loudly, many laughing. The moment she approached the stoplight, the stupid thing stuttered from her presence and went red, forcing her to wait to cross the street. A horse-drawn carriage rolled past, the couple inside sharing a kiss. Jazz blared from a bar. Several young women hung from a passing van's windows, beer bottles raised, voices loudly propositioning guys in the crowd. Several dudes followed the vehicle at a run.

Something smacked into her shoulder. Fuming, she turned.

The guy behind her laughed with his friends, their fists raised in a mock fight. Giggling, he ducked a blow, his backpack ramming into her boob.

She winced and seethed. "Hey!"

His gaze zipped over her wind-whipped hair and leather catsuit. He barked a laugh. "Halloween's over, babe. Didn't anyone tell you?"

Hurt and rage tore through her. She reached out to reap. One less Neanderthal on this planet wouldn't matter.

He glanced at her hand, his silly grin intact, male privilege oozing from him.

She should have seen red. But Rafael filled her mind, his sweet-sad eyes when she'd thrown him out of her place, his loving embrace, heated kisses, unrestrained passion and unconditional acceptance of everything she was and wasn't. An imperfect and doomed reaper.

If her body count rose again, she'd be dragging him down with her. As her PO, he was ultimately responsible for her mishaps.

She dropped her hand and darted through traffic. Horns blared. Rather than pissing her off even more, the noise soothed her. She couldn't hear the howling dogs any longer. On the other side of the street, she ran hard and long, wishing she had a direction in mind other than escape.

No matter the distance she put between herself and the service, Rafael still invaded her thoughts, her need for him endless.

By the time she circled back to her place, sun spilled over the horizon. After a warm shower and a stiff vodka nightcap, deep sleep eluded her. Fleeting dreams left behind sorrow and unease.

Come evening, she'd planned to arrive late for her shift but couldn't suffer another moment away from Rafael. Even though nothing would happen between them, she could use their remaining time together to grow stone cold again, preparing herself for his inevitable departure.

At the door, she drew in as much soggy air as she could and shuffled inside.

Heather looked up at the pulsing lights then down. She stared at Wynona's outfit—a tight leather dress with spaghetti straps. The garment laced up the front to show off her boobs. Both sides also had laces, revealing all of her legs and most of her hips. Completing her ensemble were thigh-high boots sporting four-inch heels. Everything in black.

Yeah, she knew Halloween had passed, like that douche had said last night. She happened to like her clothes, so screw him.

Heather pointed her pen at the dress. "Where'd you get that?"

"Rock Hard. Online store."

"Expensive?"

"No way. I only do cheap."

Heather beamed. "I think Daemon would like that on me for our next time at Whatever Goes."

MJ strolled past, bells tinkling. "Precious, it's Anything Goes."

"Right." Heather smiled at Wynona. "I keep getting the name wrong."

"No prob. You want to borrow this? No need to buy your own."

Heather leaned forward. "Between you and me, MJ insists I never buy anything. She wants me to wish for stuff, which she delivers faster than Amazon." Heather shook her head. "Doesn't seem right, I like to pay for or borrow things. So thanks for your offer. I'll definitely take you up on it. You feel better tonight?"

That depended on what happened when she saw Rafael again. "I'm good. Any early walk-ins I can strap down? I swear I'll be careful from now on."

"I know you will. No customers yet, but Rafael's in the break room."

Wynona's legs bowed. She gripped Heather's desk to keep from sagging to the floor. "Daemon there, too?"

"He's at home finishing his snack. I expect him in a half hour or so. Sooner if the food runs out."

"What about the three stooges?"

Heather went blank, brightened then sighed. "That's not nice."

"Neither are Anatol, Stefin or Taro, at least to me."

"They'll come around, I'm sure. They're with Zoe in her office." A scarlet stain spread from Heather's neck to her face. "Better not disturb them."

They're humping one another again. "Thanks, I wasn't planning to intrude. Call me when you need me, I'll be in my office."

"You bet."

Wynona trekked down the hall, pausing frequently to gather courage and resolve. She stopped at her office door and glanced over. Heather had left her desk. Chewing her lip, Wynona fought her urge to see Rafael. They'd be in the same room soon enough, once a customer agreed to let her within a hundred feet of him.

Her reputation for earlier mishaps had preceded her. What she'd done last night hadn't added to her appeal. Maybe she should stick to paperwork. She still had an endless amount to plow through.

She gripped the knob, released it and practically ran to the break room.

Rafael was at the refrigerator, the door open, his hair loose.

Is he deliberately trying to kill me?

Those dark, silky waves grazed his shoulders, a black shirt hugged his broad back and gray pants draped provocatively over his firm ass. He grabbed something from the top shelf, straightened and faced her.

She recalled when she'd watched him cook and he'd broken into a smile.

No grin tonight.

He regarded her outfit, blinked slowly and became aloof once more.

God help her, she missed his desire when she shouldn't. She waited for him to say something, even if it was work related or involved her fuck-ups last night.

Keeping his peace, he extended his hand and offered her the Mars bar he'd taken from the fridge. Her favorite candy, especially when chilled.

She wasn't certain whether he was simply being friendly or was trying to seduce her. Her pulse leaped. "Since when do you like Mars bars?"

"Late nineteen-thirties, early forties, I can't recall the exact year. If you want this, better take it before Daemon arrives."

She crossed the room to Rafael. He put the candy bar on the table before she could touch him. Her cheeks burned at how he avoided her, precisely as everyone else did, exactly what she'd once wanted.

He pulled out a chair.

She wasn't certain what to make of his gesture. "For me?"

"Who else?"

At this point, she hadn't a clue and dropped into the seat.

He grabbed another candy bar from the fridge and sat across the table from her. Far, far away, the doorway at his back should he need to make a fast exit. This wasn't turning out as she'd hoped. Not that she was sure what she wanted at this point, except for him to be safe from her, though not quite so remote.

He peeled the wrapper from his candy. "Did you have a good evening last night after you left here?"

There was no way she could have considering she'd screwed up so many clients and missed him like mad. She stopped nibbling her candy, aggravated at how serene he was when she was ready to jump out of her skin. "Yeah, hooked up with the Sandman."

Rafael chewed his bite, swallowed and studied his treat. "You slept well then?"

She laughed softly. "I'm not talking about going to bed, at least not alone."

He looked at her, his gaze hard and possessive.

Her nipples peaked and her cleft tingled. She should have backed off but couldn't. Yearning and loneliness drove away her good sense. She wanted a reaction from him, even if it was bad. Anything would be better than disinterest. "I'm talking about *the* Sandman, not the silly fable parents tell their children. The real one puts mortals to sleep permanently. Like I do. My kinda guy. We fit. Always have. I can't hurt him."

"You haven't hurt me...at least not until now."

Egging him on seemed incredibly stupid and cruel suddenly. Never had she been more ashamed. "I didn't mean... I shouldn't have said...I..." She jumped from her chair and crawled across the table to him.

He met her halfway.

They kissed so hard, Wynona's teeth dug into her bottom lip. She suffered the pain gladly and yanked him closer. The table bounced. He rolled them over, settling her on top. She straddled him and drove her fingers through his hair then unbuttoned his shirt and cupped his balls and rod.

Massive, hard, thick, raring to go.

Unleashed from her few inhibitions, she pushed his tongue aside and filled him with hers.

Footfalls approached and stopped outside the room.

She came to her senses fast. It wasn't right for her to do this in front of an audience, not to mention she'd already screwed up his poor wings. She broke free and scrambled off the table, skirt hiked to her upper thighs, front laces undone, left boob hanging out.

"Hmm." Stefin wiggled his eyebrows.

Taro and Anatol grinned.

She shouldered past them and sprinted toward her office. Unable to make it that far, she ducked into an empty treatment room and slumped against the table.

The door flew opened. Rafael stormed inside. His shirttails hung out, a few buttons were missing, his zipper was down and his hair hung over his forehead and eyes. He blew the locks away then shut and locked the door.

She put out her hand. "Stay there. You and I aren't going for a repeat of what just happened in the break room."

"Why not?" He planted his hands on his hips. "I don't kiss as well as the Sandman?"

She clenched her fists, ready to explode. "There is no freaking Sandman. Not in my bed, anyway. Well, not for a long time. He's history. I never even liked the turd. I was alone last night."

Rafael smiled. His handsome features became beatific.

Her insides turned to goo.

"Thank you, baby." He opened his arms and approached.

She lifted her foot, her spike heel deadly. "Not one more step unless you want an unscheduled castration. Whether you like it or not, I'm going to save you from yourself."

"By wearing that?" He gestured to her skanky outfit. Even Kim Kardashian would have been ashamed to be seen in it. "By coming into the break room?" He inched closer. "By crawling across the table to me? By sucking my tongue halfway down your throat?"

She arched one eyebrow. "I didn't hear any complaints."

"Hey, I'm just asking what's going on. You're hot one minute, cold the next."

And he wasn't?

He lifted his shoulders. "PMS?"

She growled.

After a cautious step back, he finger-combed his hair, zipped his fly and buttoned what he could of his shirt. "This has to stop."

"I couldn't agree more."

"Great. As your PO, I'm ordering you to sleep with me."

"What?"

"I outrank you. You have to do what I say. Besides, I'm a big boy. I've already asked you to corrupt me, which means I don't want you saving my butt. I want to get it on, do the thing, rock and roll."

"You mean continue with the vanilla sex we've had."

He laughed. "That's what you call vanilla?"

Actually, more like preschool when it came to carnal pleasure. He had no idea how indecent she could be. If she showed him the real Wynona, he'd surely consider her tawdry, which she was. His distaste would crush her but might save him, the only thing that mattered.

She stuffed in her boob and laced up her dress. "Ever hear of the Thin Red Line?"

"The war movie?"

"Hardly." She smoothed the leather over her stomach. "It's a nightclub for supernaturals. Lots of chains, manacles, whips, riding crops. You following?"

"Uh…"

She slunk to him, heels tapping temptingly, hips swaying. "Strange as it may seem, I like the sub role with a very strong Dom in charge." She ran her nail over his jaw. "Want to be my Master?"

He swallowed. The prominent ridge in his throat bobbed. "You mean hurt you?"

"Arouse me." She leaned in to him and wallowed in his scent. "Strip then spread me wide, shackle me so I can't move, pink up my ass, mark me as your possession. Four stripes, five, a dozen. Up to you. Display me to the audience. Take me in front of them in every possible way. Nothing forbidden. Claim me as your sexual slave, a submissive you'll use well, hard and long."

He stared. "Audience?"

"Dozens of men aching to be you as you mount me from numerous positions, using every orifice." She eased back. "You in?"

He opened his mouth then closed it.

She steeled herself for his disgust, warning herself not to cry. She'd fallen on her sword for the greater good.

He staggered back and reached blindly for the doorknob.

She lowered her face.

"Yeah, I'm in. We'll leave as soon as your shift ends."

"What? Wait." By the time she got to the door, he was already down the hall. Stefin, Anatol and Taro followed close behind.

Wynona hurried after them. Zoe shot around the corner, cutting her off. They both reared back.

"Have a question." Zoe slipped her arm through Wynona's and pulled her down the hall away from Rafael and the guys. "Heather said you're lending out your dress. Love the laces. Can I borrow it tonight? I wouldn't ask normally, but Stefin couldn't stop gushing about it. I'd put in a wish with MJ, but she likes to play with my head before giving me what I want. I'm so not in the mood tonight. After work, Stefin and the guys are taking me to the second circle. This time, I want to look slightly more demure. Keep the others guessing about what's under the leather before the boys strip me bare. So, can I? Heather said you're not pissed at us anymore. You're not, right?"

She pinched her nose. "Hold me, please?"

"Sure." Zoe hugged her. "What's wrong?"

"Do you have any information on what happens to a good angel turned bad?"

"They don't get to go to the second circle, that's for sure. You'd think they would, being corrupted and all, but Satan doesn't take kindly to traitors. Doesn't trust them like he would someone born rotten or anyone conned into selling their soul. Bastard. Don't get me started on what he did to me."

"I won't. Can good angels ever redeem themselves once they've fallen?"

"Dunno. I suppose anything's possible."

"Like me becoming mortal? Or you being alive and human again like you once were?"

"I see your point. Is this about Rafael?"

"He won't listen. He's so horny he's willing to screw up his wings, career and existence to get some action. So far, we've only made love missionary style, which is strictly for newbies, and already some of his feathers are turning black. After the Thin Red Line, those suckers will probably fall off. He won't be able to ascend to Heaven." She gripped Zoe's shoulders. "He'll be stuck here on a fast track to Hell."

"Want me to have my guys talk to him?"

"To recruit him even faster to the Dark Side?"

"Right, lost my head for a moment." She rubbed Wynona's back. "Maybe Rafael won't like what goes on once he sees it in action."

Of course, he won't, but by then it might be too late to save him.

Rafael stared at the computer screen, his mouth sagging open at the website Stefin had pulled up. It seemed there was no end to fetish wear. Cuffs, collars, gags, muzzles, blindfolds, hoods and cock harnesses danced before his eyes. Dominating those other things was something called the 'seven circles of hell D ring for cocks'. The gadget looked like a torture device from his slave days. "I'm supposed to wear stuff like this at the club?"

He'd told them about Wynona's invitation then asked for their advice on how to behave and what to wear. A huge mistake.

Stefin looked over. "Knowing Wynona, that stuff won't be hardcore enough. Hey, guys, what's that site for a Dominatrix and her boy toy?"

"Hold it." Rafael turned in his chair. "She said I'm the Master and she's the sub."

"You're sure? That doesn't sound like the pissy reaper we know."

He tightened his jaw. "Yeah, I'm exceedingly sure about what she said. And her name is Wynona, not pissy reaper or anything else pejorative, got it?"

Stefin looked at Anatol, his gaze questioning.

Anatol sighed. "Pejorative means rude, unkind, nasty."

Stefin nodded and held up his hands to Rafael. "Easy, all right? If she's the sub, that changes everything. You can wear what we usually do at the BDSM clubs."

A long red cape materialized, the garment suspended in air. Beside it hung black tights, the front and back parts cut out to expose a man's cock, balls and ass. There were also boots that laced up the front and a wide belt with a whip hanging from it.

Rafael thought the leather pants Stefin had put him in were awful. He pointed at the items. "That's as bad, possibly worse, than what's on the site. I'll look ridiculous."

"Hot." Stefin winked.

Taro and Anatol snickered.

"Are you guys putting me on? I know I'm an easy target."

They sobered. Taro shook his head. "We're not yanking your chain. Doms wear stuff like this at the clubs."

"What about subs? What will Wynona wear?"

Stefin smiled. "A ball gag for sure."

"What's that?"

"This." His fingers flew over the keyboard.

What he brought up wasn't any better than the first site, except this one catered to females. Rafael made a face at a red rubber ball shoved into a woman's mouth and held there by straps. "Why would Wynona want to wear that?"

"She wouldn't. You'd want that to keep her quiet."

Rafael bunched his shoulders. "Care to rephrase that?"

"Hey, she's your babe, do whatever you want. Leave me out of it." Stefin stepped back.

Rafael perused the site, checking out lockdown cinchers, spanking panties and half-cup leather bras. He increased the zoom. The bras were nice. Up next were chastity thongs, riding crops, studded paddles and bullwhips. *That can't be fun.* Also represented were collars, wrist and ankle restraints, arm binders, spreader bars, long black gloves and jeweled masks. *She'd look good in one of those babies. But the rest...* "Do women really like this?"

"Don't knock it 'til you've tried it." Anatol leaned down and typed something. "Check this out."

A video started, music swelled, the strains dark though more smoldering than ominous. The photography was surprisingly professional and the lighting was sensuous. A dozen black candles cast a soft glow on a stone wall that resembled one found in an ancient monastery or dungeon. Thick chains dangled from the ceiling and ended in brutal manacles. Two bolts were in the floor, spaced widely apart. Secured to them were shackles. The metal glinted dully in the faint light.

Drums beat. The booming sounds introduced a huge dude who strutted into the scene. He wore a full hood, lace-up boots, a leather belt and those ridiculous cut-out tights. His schlong was at least twelve inches and dangled halfway down his thigh.

One of the guys bumped Rafael's arm. He didn't bother to see which one, unable to tear his attention away from the screen. The dude's, or rather the Master's, balls were larger than ripe plums.

The percussion grew frenzied. A woman, the presumed sub, wiggled into the scene, her high-heel boots similar to what Wynona usually wore, only these were even higher. She had on the red cape.

Rafael smacked his palm against the desk. "I knew you guys were putting me on. That's women's wear."

Taro shook his head. "Unisex. A Dom or female sub can wear it. Watch."

Already, the Master had secured his sub's arms above her head and her ankles to the floor, which spread her legs widely. The camera angle changed, showing her from the front. She'd lowered her head. Long blonde curls hid her face. She whimpered.

Stefin huddled close. "Ball-gag time."

Sure enough, the Master pulled one off a nearby table, this ball in black.

The sub shook her head vigorously. "I'll be good."

Stefin made a derisive sound.

The Master tossed the gag back on the table, untied the cape and pulled it off her.

Rafael gripped the desk. Leather strips crisscrossed her curves, a kind of harness that didn't cover her boobs, ass or cleft in the least. Like Wynona, she had no hair down there. Gold rings hung from her folds and nipples. Another dangled from the wide black collar around her throat.

Violins played. Her downcast eyes completed her submissive position.

The drumming resumed, trumpets wailed, cymbals crashed. The Master kept his cool, strolling around her, tapping the whip against his palm. She looked over. He growled. Head down, she waited for her punishment.

The music cut off. The only sound now was Rafael's heavy breathing. The guys', too. They crowded him, their attention riveted to the screen.

The Master lifted his arm.

The ends of the whip jumped.

A drumroll rang out.

He brought the whip down.

The scene changed to slo-mo, the camera showing a close-up of the sub's satiny ass. The knotted cords struck the middle of her butt cheeks and curled around her hip.

She keened. A wailing trumpet accompanied her.

Four times, the Master meted out her punishment, leaving new marks in different areas. Finished, he dropped the whip and buried his face in her cunt, licking her lust-drenched folds.

She cried out.

He squeezed her whipped cheeks and gorged on her clit, not allowing her to come. She clenched her fists and fought her restraints. For her disobedience, she got another lick from the whip.

Perspiration shone on her neck, torso and back.

The Master explored the separation between her cheeks and her anus. She pushed to her toes. For that response, he tightened the ceiling chains, ensuring she remained in the position. Stretched out, trapped, used.

He drew the whip between her legs, stroked her nub with the handle and kissed her deeply.

She surrendered anew, arched her back to expose her breasts and pushed them into his palms.

The drums started again. Maybe they'd never stopped, Rafael couldn't be certain.

The Master undid the ankle shackles.

That didn't seem right. "Is it over?"

"Nope." Anatol pointed at the screen. "Watch."

With her feet free, the Master pulled her legs up to his hips and drove his gargantuan cock into her dripping sheath. Her head fell back. He kissed her throat, pumped like a mad man for five full minutes and finally came.

The video went black.

Rafael wilted in his chair, winded as though he'd run miles, his rod so hard the skin stung. Well on his way to corruption.

Chapter Nine

Once her shift began, Wynona rushed through her clients without major incident. Each time she had a spare moment, she hotfooted it to her office and scoured the net for information about good angels turning bad then back again.

Google claimed to have all the data in the universe. *Ha.* The only stuff that popped up on her screen was from paranormal TV shows, phony spiritualists looking to make a fast buck, chatrooms populated with the clueless or trolls with snarky comments.

She was on her own. *Surprise, surprise.*

When the last client exited, she handed her dress over to Zoe. It was too long but the overall effect was dazzling. "You totally rock that."

Zoe smiled shyly, the flames in her eyes demure. "No, I don't. I'm not you."

"Thank your lucky stars for that."

"What are you talking about? You're gorgeous, tall and built. If I'd looked like you when I was mortal, I wouldn't have sold my soul for Ebenezer's love, which by the way, didn't work out. Prick."

"I'm sorry. You really envy me?"

"What woman wouldn't?"

"Try all of them. I'm a reaper."

Zoe shrugged. "You come off as a hardass, but you're actually a pussycat inside. I'd chalk up a lot of your problems to women being envious of you."

"What about the way men avoid me?"

"They have problems I couldn't begin to get into."

She had a point. Rafael had just arrived to pick Wynona up for their *date*. Prom night this wasn't. Black tights hugged his sinewy thighs and calves. His feet were clad in retro combat boots. A macho belt hung from his lean hips, a mean-looking whip dangling from it. His chest was bare, shoulders covered by a full-length black cape. His junk hung free, his cock on the move, rising to point at her, his nuts puffing up.

Despite her misgivings about this, her folds grew plump and damp. She wasn't only doomed, she was damned.

Zoe looked over. "Guess I should go." She zipped out of the room.

Rafael eyed the black terrycloth robe Wynona wore, 'From Crud to Stud' embroidered in red on the front. The service gave these as parting gifts to clients who'd graduated the programs. It was also a clever marketing ploy to get the brand out to others.

He gestured to the robe. "You're going to the club in that?"

She gestured right back at him. "Are you kidding me with what you're wearing?"

His face darkened. "Doms dress like this all the time."

"Who told you that? Stefin?"

Rafael's cheeks flushed. "Taro said the red cape was unisex. Who cares? I refuse to wear anything but black." He smoothed the garment. "The red one's still in the treatment room. You can wear it."

"Now you're telling me how to dress?"

"As your PO, I should have." He stroked the whip. "As your Dom, I have the right."

The pulse within her pussy beat harder. Her folds were dripping. She shouldn't like him this way, considering it was screwing up his future, but it was murder to resist. Also necessary if she expected him to come out of this relatively unscathed.

She drew back her shoulders. "You're not my Dom until we get to the club. I'm going home to change first. You can wait here."

He blocked her. "I'll take you."

"Don't trust that I'll come back?"

"I know you will." He fingered her robe. "I want to see you get dressed." He tugged the terrycloth. "As soon as you lose this, we'll go."

She was nude underneath, except for her boots. "You expect me to leave here without clothes."

"Like I said, I'll take you." He unfurled his wings.

They were wider and longer than she recalled. Darker, too. Black marched through white. She reeled.

He untied the sash around her waist, eased off the robe and pulled her close. Their fronts molded together, his rigid shaft sheltered between her slick folds. She gripped his arms to keep upright. Her throat convulsed from too many emotions.

"Everything will be all right." He brushed his lips over her cheek. "I promise."

"How? Nothing that involves us will ever be okay."

"Trust me, it will. I want this. I want you." He captured her mouth, spearing his tongue deep.

Her knees bumped his. Their lips melded, his kiss impassioned and starved for her, the same as she was for him.

They ascended through the ceiling and roof to the outside, invisible as the last time.

Which meant he could slip back into Heaven without anyone seeing him. That might solve his wing problem. He could retract those suckers and keep them hidden with no one being the wiser.

She eased her mouth from his. "Do you do this when you go home?"

He tensed, his grip tightening around her waist. "Kiss women?"

No, but now she was curious. "Sure. We'll go with that. Do you?"

"Only Ursula. She's history, like your Sandman."

"He's not mine. Do you go home invisible like we are now?"

"Until I reach the security gates."

"They're not pearly like I've heard?"

"Things change. Too many trying to storm the castle, so to speak. We have face and voice recognition now, along with retinal scanning, iris recognition, cavity searches and full-body X-rays before anyone can put one toe in the place."

Sounded horrible and didn't make sense. "Given what's happened to your wings, how'd you get through the last time when you picked up a change of clothes and our breakfast?"

"My feathers hadn't turned yet. Must have been a delayed reaction."

One he was making up for now, barreling full steam toward destruction. "What's the matter with your people? Whatever happened to trust?"

"The last financial meltdown proved what a mistake that was. I can't tell you the guys who're on St. Peter's shit list now."

She didn't care about them, only him. Those endless security measures brought her right back to the original plan—repulsing him with her true nature before he lost his chance to forego corruption and repented.

So be it. She was up to the task.

Once in her apartment, Wynona rummaged through her clothes, searching for her most disgraceful outfit. A tough choice since there were more than a few.

Rafael gazed longingly at the bed and bath where they'd had so much fun and the chair they'd snuggled on while sharing breakfast. His face brimmed with hope, no different from a mortal who still longed for a miracle.

There wouldn't be one tonight. For them to stay here wrapped in each other's needs wasn't possible. He had to witness the horrible truth about her and reform.

She shoved one garment after the other aside. Hangers rattled on the iron pole.

He glanced away, face down.

She blinked back tears and found what she needed. It didn't take her long to get dressed given her scanty outfit. Bracing herself for the worst, she spoke. "I'm ready."

Her military-style jacket sported a high collar and long sleeves, had no zipper or buttons, barely covered the sides of her breasts and stopped well above her fake navel. She'd seated a large rhinestone in the depression.

Her half-cup leather bra lifted her boobs and exposed her nipples. Gold rings hung from each.

She'd paired her crotchless thong with a lacy garter belt that held up sheer black stockings, had donned her boots once more and wore a slave collar around her throat. The leather was savagely wide and studded with gold rings so her Master could easily slip a chain or his finger through the hoops from the front, back, right or left to yank her toward him. Making certain she behaved.

In order to put even more emotional distance between them, she'd slipped on a full-face mask in black satin, adorned with lace, sequins and feathers. Sheer material covered the eye openings, allowing her to see out, while keeping him from seeing in and gauging her emotions. Given how her mouth was covered, he couldn't claim her lips. No matter what anyone thought or said, a kiss was far more intimate than sex.

As her Dom, he'd have full access to her body tonight but nothing else.

Most men would have been turning cartwheels or groping her lewdly. He ignored her raunchy costume and stared at her eyes. "Take off the mask."

"No. It's part of my costume."

"I don't like it."

"I do."

"I'm your Dom."

"Not 'til we get to the club."

He grabbed her wrist and pulled her into him. "Fine. Off we go."

"You're going to be sorry."

Rafael cupped her ass and squeezed her cheeks. "Wrong. You'll be sorry if you don't behave." He pressed his mouth to the sensitive area beneath her ear and sucked.

She collapsed against him, scarcely able to think. "While we're there, beat my butt good. Screw me raw. I don't want to disappoint the audience."

He stilled and straightened. "Hurt me if you must, but I won't change my mind."

Damn him for being so sweet and vulnerable. She needed him to be more like Marquis de Sade. If Rafael refused to toughen up, she would. "How in the hell could I even get close to hurting you when you're doing such a bang-up job on your own?"

He frowned. "I should have listened to Stefin."

"Let me guess, he's been talking up Hell and how great it'll be when your ass lands there."

"He advised me to use a ball gag on you. Silly me, I said no way and told him to watch his mouth about you or else."

Rafael was too wonderful for her or any woman, even a good angel. She pressed her forehead to his shoulder. Her mask dented. "Thanks."

He stroked her back. "Let's not argue. Tell you what, we can stay here tonight. After we play around, I'll make dinner or breakfast, whatever you want."

Satan couldn't have tempted Wynona more if he'd offered her a chance to be a teenybopper, experiencing life, friendship and acceptance followed by a ticket to Heaven for eternity. None of that meant anything now. Her love for Rafael was paramount and gave her the courage to resist his wonderful suggestion and pull away. "Too vanilla. Boring in comparison to the club. Stay here if you want. I can go alone."

He caught her hand. "Let's cut to the chase. Tell me you hate me and I'll leave. Tell me you haven't liked me for a moment and I'll never bother you again."

"Wow, bingo on both. You are perceptive."

"Say the words, Wynona."

She should have but couldn't get her mouth to work.

"Exactly as I thought." With a gentle smile, he pulled her back into him. "How much cash should I bring for the cover charge?"

"You have money?"

"All POs have bank accounts for incidental expenses."

"Like taking parolees to BDSM clubs?"

"How much will I need to withdraw tonight?"

"Keep it. I have a running tab there and at a dozen other places. What can I say? I'm a hedonist with nympho tendencies."

She smiled proudly, waiting for him to bolt.

His cock wiggled against her. "Hang on." He soared through the ceiling. "Where is this dive? I'm guessing not up. Should I go down?"

She gave him directions.

The club was within a recently inactive volcano, its entrance carved through a slit in the blackened rock. Fiery embers glowed around the edges. Thus the name, the Thin Red Line, which also referred to marks left by Doms on subs' asses.

The moment they landed, Wynona grabbed Rafael's arm to keep him from going inside. "Retract your wings. Anyone sees your remaining white feathers and I'll have to reap as I've never done before so no one tears you apart."

"You'd destroy others for me?"

If she were able to bite the dust, she'd die for him. "I may be a reaper, but I have some honor. You're fresh meat here. Better listen to mama."

He tucked those sweet things in, slipped his finger through a side ring on her collar and tugged her forward. "Don't keep me waiting."

"I won't, oh, glorious, wondrous, stupendous Master."

Rafael looked over. "Lose the 'tude." He turned her around and smacked her butt.

Heat raced through her. She wanted him to paddle her again and give her several screaming orgasms.

He pulled her inside the volcano.

Smoke billowed toward them, the sulfur stench more pungent than Zoe and her guys. Jagged rocks shimmered red and black. White flashes zigzagged on the ceiling and walls, resembling lightning streaked across a night sky. Thunderous music pounded. The alternative beat mixed metal, punk, grunge and whatever else the band could throw together.

A leviathan of a guy blocked the club entrance, his black hood hiding his features, eyes narrowed, lips pressed together, his getup the same as Rafael's, his dong too big to be real. It was either enhanced by magic or he was a shifter, possibly a mule or a horse.

As soon as Rafael spotted the dude, he stopped.

Wynona's hope soared. "It's okay if you want to go back to the service or Heaven. I can't blame you. This is nuts."

"I know that guy."

That wasn't possible. His face was covered. "He's your old slave master? You fought him in a battle of good and evil? You're his PO, too?"

"Next time I'm bringing a ball gag."

With that attitude, there won't be a next time. "Excuse me?"

"He was in a video Anatol pulled up." Rafael hurried to the guy, yanking her with him. "Hey, good job with the blonde in the monastery or dungeon. Please tell me that wasn't the only recording you made."

Mr. Colossus smiled sweetly. "Dungeon. I have a string of videos. Hold on." He grabbed a backpack from the floor, dug in it and pulled out a business card. "My website addy's on here." He handed the card over. "I'm doing this job in between gigs. BDSM acting is a tough business. Pirates are screwing me royally by putting my stuff online for free. Hey, I gotta eat and pay rent like everyone else."

Nodding solemnly, Rafael tucked the card beneath his belt. "Anything of yours I watch from now on, I promise to buy first."

He pointed. "No sharing, either."

"Never. You have my word."

Wynona tugged on her collar. The leather bit into her throat, cutting off her scream at this idiotic conversation. Rafael shouldn't watch porn. No wonder his wings were worse than the last time she'd seen them.

He pulled her into him and turned to the guy. "About the cover charge."

"No biggie." He stepped aside. "Tonight's on me. Enjoy."

They gave each other a high-five.

Rafael pulled her down the smoky passage. "You're sure you have a tab here? He didn't seem to recognize you."

"I'm wearing a mask."

"Not any longer." He pulled it off and tucked it into his belt.

She licked sweat off her upper lip. "Don't crush my feathers."

"You seem to have forgotten who the Dom is." Using his superior height and weight, he backed her into the stone, his lips on hers, hands cupping her boobs. He played with the rings in her nipples and drove his tongue so deep within her mouth she couldn't make a noise. If she had, the sound would have betrayed how much she enjoyed him as a Master, PO, man, lover and friend.

Her plan was tanking badly, but she couldn't seem to get on track, too lost in pleasure, warmth bombarding her. She cradled his silky cock, the column rock hard. More heat poured from it than a furnace. Heedlessly, she stroked the most sensitive part on his crown.

He juddered and pushed her hand away.

She brought it right back.

On a rough growl, he pulled his mouth from hers. "You need to behave, I mean it."

"No, you don't. Not unless you're ready to discipline me with a whip, cane, crop or all three."

His color drained.

What do you know, I've found his Achilles' heel. He may have talked big while they'd been at the office and played the Dom part before they'd gotten into the club. However, meting out punishment was another matter.

"As you wish." He grabbed her collar ring and pulled her forward.

She should have run in the other direction rather than tremble with excitement. "You don't know where to go."

He stopped and looked over. "Behind us is Yardley. The club's in front of us. There aren't any detours. We're going in the right direction."

"What or who is Yardley?"

"The bouncer, video guy. Come on."

After a short walk, they entered a cavernous area. Candles in the hundreds barely ate away the shadows. This was only the first room of many in the club. The mildest, too, for newbies.

A circular stage dominated the center area. Torches lit the wooden frame and glinted off the chains and manacles at the top for wrists, the bottom for ankles. Nearby were straps and paddles.

Rafael stared at a table to the side. A were was bent over the top, ass raised, a woman between his thighs, an impressive dildo secured to the belt around her hips. Red marks crisscrossed her plush ass.

Like a good little sub, she'd see to her Dom's pleasure now.

At the other tables, vamps, reapers, demons and shifters flogged each other, screwed like maniacs, enjoyed their drinks or ate seared steaks, prime rib, stuffed chops, barbeque pork and countless meat variations while waiting for the main attraction—a Dom displaying his or her sub on stage, punishing then leaving that person spread-eagled and chained so others could squeeze the sub's whipped cheeks and suck nipples, clits, balls or cocks.

Rafael's was fully erect, so hard the damn thing pointed at his head. If he got any more excited, he'd pass out.

"Do we grab our own table?" He glanced around. "Or is there a maître d'?"

He was worse than green at this, more like blinding white. "We need to move on."

"Why?"

"Too tame in here."

He took in the stage and the fornicating crowd, his head practically spinning on his shoulders like the kid in *The Exorcist*.

The next room was more intimate, no chairs or tables, just beds. Chained to the head and footboards were men and women, facedown or up, depending on how their Doms preferred to discipline them.

One guy had clamps on his nipples and balls. He begged for more. His Dom clamped the head of his cock. Rafael shuddered and dragged Wynona to another bed. There, a brunette was on all fours, head bowed, ass lifted to her Dom—a huge black guy with a killer smile, a dimple carved into one cheek and flames in his eyes. He squeezed her whipped ass. Her butt cheeks practically glowed red.

She moaned. "More, please."

He squirted a pinkish lotion over the scarlet marks and rubbed. She shouted and squirmed, unable to get too far away. Thick chains held her in place.

Her Dom growled. "Keep still."

She sniffled and settled. He rubbed the concoction on her again, a pepper-and-salt mixture Wynona was more than familiar with. The sub recoiled from the burning sting then pressed closer, her moan ecstatic.

Rafael looked at Wynona, his eyebrows raised in question.

She shook her head. "Too tame."

In the next chamber, subs were chained to the walls. Queued-up Doms stepped from one to the other like an assembly line, meting out their punishments with paddles, canes, whips and riding crops. Cries and moans choroused in the heated air. Staffers served beer or mixed drinks to the Doms. The subs earned a sip of water if they got through three swats without shrieking or crying then *begged* for more of the same.

Few remained quiet in this room. It was an exceedingly popular area.

Rafael drank everything in, his eyes as wide as hers had probably been when she'd reaped her first soul. "This can't be too tame."

"It is."

He rubbed his temple. "Maybe you should show me what you had in mind."

"Not liking this, huh?"

He gave her a look and gestured to his cock that not only pointed at his head but also left a dent in his belly from being so hard.

Her stupid plan wasn't only failing, it was backfiring badly. Not one to give up, she gestured him forward. "Come on."

He pulled her back. "I refuse to hurt you."

"No pain, no gain."

"Be serious."

"Do you see me laughing? This is who I am. If you don't want to discipline me, fine, I'll pay someone else. You can watch. Let's go."

He yanked her back. "No one's touching you except me." He stroked her cheek.

She should have torn away but couldn't.

They were getting in deeper by the second and she only had the coming minutes to convince him how wrong he was to want her. *How screwed up is that?* Since her existence had begun, she'd hoped for someone who'd stick with her no matter what. No one had answered her prayers. Fucking fate had brought Rafael to her instead, giving her two impossible options. No, three. Hurt him, herself, or both of them.

She waved down a server. He was naked like the others, except for his collar, a harness around his shoulders and an extender on his cock, guaranteed to add two inches to a guy's length. If the pain didn't kill him first.

His face was red, shoulders drawn in. Despite his bright color, his fangs showed. A vamp.

Poor thing was in misery. "Hurting?"

"It's worth it. Once I'm long enough, I get a bump in pay."

Amazing what folks go through for money, even supernaturals. "Is the Double B free?"

"All yours. Want us to make an announcement or do you plan on an intimate date?" He slid his gaze to Rafael and licked his fangs.

Wynona smacked the vamp's arm to get his attention. "Make an announcement. The more the merrier."

"Hold on." Rafael frowned. "No announcement."

"This is who I am."

He tightened his jaw.

"Go on." She flicked her hand at the vamp. "Do as I said." She spoke to Rafael. "If you don't want to do this, you can—"

"I'm not leaving, I'm not handing you over to someone else and I'm not going to discuss this with you any longer. What's the Double B?"

"The room we're going to. Double B is a nickname we use."

"What's the proper name?"

"Bucking Bronco."

"I'm not following."

Few good angels would.

"Attention, attention, attention."

Rafael glanced up at the voice coming over the sound system.

"We have a treat tonight. The Double B is booked."

Hoots and hollers rose. A few dudes dashed toward the room.

Rafael looked at her, confusion in his eyes.

She wanted to hug him but kept her distance. "It's easier for me to show you than explain."

He trudged after her, not acting like a Dom any longer, forgetting to be *the man*. It sucked to do this to him, but she had no choice.

In the candlelit room, fifty or more supernaturals waited, all male. Some cradled plates piled high with their dinners. Others held drinks. Their chairs circled a large ebony statue of a horse, its head thrown back, hindquarters down. Protruding from the neck was a phallus easily reached by a rider's mouth if she bent at the waist and leaned forward. She'd have to in order to raise her ass for punishment. The cock was to keep her from crying out.

Two more phalluses jutted from the saddle, one for a woman's pussy, the other to fill her anus and confine her during discipline. Riding crops, whips, canes and paddles hung from hooks bored into the stone wall. A huge mirror on the right reflected the scene so the sub could witness her chastisement, the Dom her reaction.

Rafael stared.

Chapter Ten

Wynona waited as long as she could for Rafael to scream at her or take off. When he did neither, she had no choice except to make a move. The audience was getting unruly. Feet smacked the floor, grunts and growls rocketed through the room. In a few more seconds, the guys would battle each other to take Rafael's place as her Dom. After her punishment, the braver ones, or those no longer alive, might want to mount her.

That scene had played out here in the past. What would happen next was anyone's guess, but it sure as hell wouldn't be pretty.

She shrugged out of her jacket, waved it above her head and tossed it into the crowd, her lavender scent rolling toward them. Several spectators leaped to catch her garment and bumped each other's shoulders or elbows. A fight broke out in the back row, the reapers yanking each other's hair and shrieking like teenage girls battling over a boy. Two burly bouncers rushed inside to restore order.

Wynona glanced at Rafael's reflection. His complexion was tinged with gray, features stony, erection massively thick and hard. If he was repulsed, it wasn't by this room or her but his arousal. Part of her worried he hadn't fled, while another part was grateful that he'd accepted who she was and wasn't.

No way would she ever be good like him.

The guys smacked their feet again, demanding more action than her seesawing emotions.

A vamp in front hissed lustily.

A demon shot up. Flames blazed in his black eyes. He pointed at her. "Ditch the clothes and climb on."

"Not on the horse." A reaper stroked his erection. "On this bad boy."

Everyone talked at once, bitching about what they wanted.

Rafael cracked his whip. "Quiet."

His roar cut through the whining like a laser through butter. The creatures fell silent, their attention zipping from him to her and back, respect in their eyes. A little fear, too.

Her passion revved to a dangerous level. She'd had no idea Rafael could be so commanding. He'd been such a sweetheart with her.

No more. He tapped the whip in his palm, gaze raking over her, brutal need on his face. Showtime had arrived.

Strangely bashful, she took her time removing her garter belt and easing down her thong. The satin and lace clung to her damp skin. Once she pulled off the dainty thing, Rafael put out his hand. She dropped the underwear in his palm, her fingers trembling.

Murmurs rippled through the audience.

Rafael buried his face in the thong and inhaled deeply, taking in her scent. Applause broke out. He glanced over. Everyone fell silent, though some did lean forward in their chairs. He ignored the lot, making them and her wait for his next move while he indulged. Pre-cum seeped from his cock. Bold and unashamed, he stroked the silky fluid over the head, on the fast track to absolute corruption.

Her worry jacked up harder than before.

Finished, he tied her thong to his belt and pointed his whip at her boobs. Her nipples had already peaked. Now, they stung.

Dutifully, she unclasped her bra and her breasts fell free. The steamy air in here wasn't nearly as hot as his gaze.

A lone whistle, low and lingering, flowed through the room. Numerous guys raised their hands, encouraging her to toss the bra. She gave it to Rafael, her Master, her only love.

After this was over, she'd find a way to break into Heaven and talk to his superiors, confess how she'd bought wishes, used potions and spells, even poisoned his food and drink to destroy his purity. She'd keep at it until they relented, invited him back into the fold and condemned her to hard time in Hell.

Before she began her sentence, she'd convince Constance to remove his memories of these hours. Then he could return to Ursula and their corny romance, no worse for the wear.

Though bummed, Wynona was also determined to enjoy her last moments with him. She stood mostly naked and completely defenseless, awaiting his command, wanting his strong hand as much as she did his tender kisses.

Nothing was soft about him tonight. Slowly, he circled, stopped in front and eased his whip between her legs. The cords skimmed and tickled the backs of her knees. She didn't dare giggle or move, uncertain what he might do. The crowd ate their food more quickly, downed their drinks and lifted the empty glasses or bottles for another round. Their hunger and thirst proved how much they were enjoying this. Servers weaved in and out, delivering booze. Rafael pressed the whip handle against her thighs, wordlessly commanding her to spread them.

A familiar ache settled in her pussy, which was already congested with heat and desire. She slid her feet apart, exposing herself further.

He circled to the back, ran the handle down the furrow between her cheeks and tarried on her anus.

She locked her knees to keep steady.

The server she'd spoken to earlier padded to where she and Rafael stood. The guy carried a silver tray heaped with phalluses in varying thicknesses. The attached gold chains helped keep those tools in place once inserted into an orifice. There was also a container of heavy-duty lube.

She knew what that meant and shivered in anticipation.

The server leaned toward Rafael. "These are on the house, to stretch her anus for the horse."

The audience erupted in wolf whistles and applause.

Rafael stroked the thickest device then settled his gaze on her. No smile. No softness. Just hard Dom. "Bend over, ass lifted."

The room spun. Two servers hauled in a small table for her to use as support, which she did, gripping the edge. After placing the phallus next to her where she couldn't miss it, Rafael waved the staffers away and tossed his whip on the table.

The thing clack-clacked.

She flinched.

He dipped his fingers in the lube and rested his hand on her ass. Perspiration rolled down her cheek, excitement and disquiet flooding her. Arousal won. She grasped the table harder and lifted her buttocks.

Rafael tended her.

The lube was slippery and wonderfully cool on her fevered flesh. He worked his finger into her anus, oiling her good. She made a grateful noise. Quickly, he swatted her butt, his message loud and clear. He'd tolerate no sounds from her unless he allowed them.

Wynona bit her lip and held back a delighted squeal.

He slathered the phallus with the lube, close enough for her to watch, his strokes slow, building her anticipation.

Rustling noises rose from the audience — guys shifting in their seats or leaning forward to see better. A few cleared their throats. None uttered a word.

Rafael held her anus apart with one hand and worked the phallus into the narrow passage with the other. The pressure was so insane and sinfully wicked that her jaw dropped. Fully enslaved, she relaxed as much as possible to ease his task.

He worked her with surprising expertise for a good angel and finished with the flared end flush against her opening. It stretched her mercilessly, the chains skimming her thighs. She shuddered and pulled in another shallow breath, unable to manage more. He draped the chains over her hips to her stomach and secured them beneath her bejeweled navel. With his thighs pressed against hers, he confined her further and stroked her clit.

Pleasure and heat unlike any she'd known shot through her, exploding into pure bliss. Her scalp and teeth tingled. She gasped.

Feet slapped the floor and chair legs scraped, the guys edging closer.

Rafael straightened and backed away from her. She waited for his bellow telling everyone to clear out, leaving her and him to themselves. Unless he'd finally come to his senses and was ready to take off.

She held her breath and glanced at Rafael's reflection.

He faced the other guys, his eyes hooded, his breathing hard. "Those who want a closer look can come up here and get their fill."

Her pulse jumped at his unexpected comment. She didn't know what to think.

"One by one, though." He pointed. "No touching. Break that rule at your own peril."

The line formed immediately, the guys holding their hands behind their backs like docile choirboys.

The mirror showed Rafael concentrating on the BDSM tools hanging from the wall. He stroked a cane and a riding crop while she cooled her heels and entertained the troops.

They grinned and leered.

Never had she felt as exposed or been as wet. For a newly sullied angel, Rafael had some amazing moves. That porn film must have been quite the tutorial and a bad decision on his part. Now she'd really have to pour on the charm with his superiors when she tried to extricate him from this mess. She lowered her head.

"No." He strode to her. "Face lifted, eyes on the mirror to see them look at every intimate part of you."

Her cheeks couldn't have gotten hotter. A hunky demon bent at the waist and studied her impaled ass. Her chest grew wonderfully warm. Even her nipple rings heated up.

Rafael selected a long paddle with holes in it to eliminate drag and increase thrust. He whacked the thing against the table.

She jumped.

He couldn't have looked more serene or imposing. "Everyone back to their seats."

A were stood his ground, shoulders pulled back. Rafael crowded him, his glare lethal. The guy pivoted and hurried to his chair.

Rafael returned to the table. "Do I need to gag you?"

Another squeal rose in her throat, ready to break free. However, she shook her head.

"Not one sound or word, got it? You'll not only accept my punishment, you'll crave it."

She already did.

He pointed the paddle at the mirror. "Watch for each lick. Anticipate and raise your ass to greet every one."

Damn, he was way past hot, clear to the other side of fan-fucking-tastic. She looked at the mirror.

He pushed the cape over his shoulders and affected a conqueror's stance—feet apart, back straight as an iron rod, his sex brazenly hard and irresistible. Focused on her ass, he lifted the paddle.

The hair in his pit was dark and silky, his chest glazed with perspiration, muscles corded. Hell, he was better than a god. He was Master of the freaking universe.

He whisked the paddle down.

Air whistled through the holes.

The thing connected with her right cheek, producing a loud *thwack*.

She froze at the blow, not feeling a thing. Hold it, she did, the sting rough and deep. Wincing, she stared at her reflection, eyes rounded, face ruddy, teeth clenched against a wail and a sigh as warmth washed over her, replacing the hurt.

She lifted her ass to welcome the next lick.

Rafael felt as if he were having an out-of-body experience or had stumbled into an erotic twilight zone. He stared at Wynona's ass, her milky skin pink from the paddle. His balls twitched. He glanced at his reflection, not recognizing the beast staring back at him—hair in disarray, pupils dilated, chest heaving, lacy underwear tied to his belt, cock hardened enough to hurt.

He'd never looked as good. She looked even better. Soft, feminine and yielding. Who would have thought he'd like this and would crave more? Not as a steady diet, but an occasional detour from their vanilla lovemaking, which they'd always return to. Nothing could compete with real intimacy, tenderness and belonging to another person who wouldn't judge.

After tonight, there'd be no going back to Heaven for him. His feathers were probably already solid black—maybe corroded too, if the odd twitches in his back were any indication. If they turned to ash, he didn't care except for how that would affect Wynona. She'd blame herself when he was responsible.

Maybe there was a place somewhere where they could be together and belong. Like what Maria and Tony sang about in *West Side Story*. A beautiful tune that hadn't helped their romance. Poor Tony had died before they'd even had a second date. *What a downer.*

Rafael frowned. He and Wynona would have their happily ever after...somehow.

She wiggled her ass.

He stroked the phallus base, along with her sensitive flesh. She sighed breathily. Male authority pulsed through him as it never had before. Her submission was so empowering, he couldn't believe he'd lived without this or her. No more. He brought the paddle down. Its crack rang through the room.

She arched her back.

The guys pounded their feet and applauded.

Rafael should have told them to leave. This was wrong on so many levels. Yet, their presence excited him, not that he'd let anyone get too familiar. He shot a warning glare for them not to budge from their seats.

Saints couldn't have been more reserved.

Rafael swatted her four extra times, twice on each cheek to make things even and tossed the paddle. Two guys jumped up to catch it. The winner pressed his face to the business end of the tool. *Hoping to catch her scent?*

Her enticing musk and sweet lavender enveloped Rafael, coaxing him closer, as deep as a man could go. For him, even that wouldn't be far enough. She was part of him, had been from the moment they'd met. More necessary than honor, righteousness, purity or salvation.

He mounted and drove his shaft into her pussy. They moaned together. She pushed her ass into him, taking his last inches inside. Dizzy, he leaned down and laced his fingers through hers. "You all right?"

"Is it possible to die from happiness?"

He chuckled. "I don't think so. Want to try?"

"I'm game. Don't stop, please."

For her, never. Not even if the Big Guy showed up and ordered Rafael away. He'd risk everlasting obliteration for a second more to indulge in her softness and heat.

He kissed her hairline, released her hands and pumped lazily despite his ringing ears and aching rod. Each stroke threatened to send him over the edge. Heaviness and tension built too quickly in his balls.

One guy held up a smartphone. Two others followed. "Hey." A bouncer pointed at them. "No recordings."

Good man and a great move. Rafael figured the second his lust-filled grimace and Wynona's dazed smile hit Facebook or YouTube, they'd be shit out of luck. Heaven checked those sites for vulnerable souls. Could be Becca did the same to see what her staff were up to.

Wynona tightened her sheath around his cock, urging him to go faster and harder. He brushed her clit. She whimpered. They rocked in time, lost in a primal dance meant for them alone.

She came first, crying wildly.

He resisted his release and pulled out, his cock rigid as hell, slick with her juices. Guys in the back row stood and craned their necks to see better.

The server with the torture device on his cock hurried over. "Are you through? Need a chair?"

"Not for a long time. I'll let you know."

He nodded and scooted away.

Rafael unclasped the chains around her hips, removed the phallus and buried his cock in her anus.

She shivered and made a satisfied noise.

Her heat and snug fit astonished him to an unimaginable level. He roared intentionally, proving to her how lost in pleasure he was and his endless hope for their future.

Here and now, anything seemed possible. He wasn't asking for limitless power, cruel revenge or all the riches in the world, simply time with her. Such a small request. A chance to be happy, loved, cherished and to give the same, honoring her through eternity.

How could anyone deny them that or think this was wrong? Intolerance was for mortals, not angels, right?

He wanted to be sure but wasn't, his uncertainty stoking his impossible need. Someone groaned. Might have been him. He worked her clit and thrust with unparalleled desire, forcing them to the edge, pushing them past resistance.

She tumbled first, her sweet cries exciting and soothing, making him feel worthy. His gasps and proud bellow rumbled through the room. Together they descended. This time, she laced her fingers through his, keeping him close and inside.

Where he belonged.

Their contented silence grew. Muffled coughs and murmurs sounded from the audience. Someone padded closer. Rafael bit back his frustration and opened one eye.

The same server lifted his shoulders. "Is it over now?"

Never, as far as I'm concerned. He squeezed her fingers. "Everyone out."

"Excuse me?"

"Beat it. Now."

"Yes, Sir."

"Wait." Rafael lifted his head. "After everyone leaves, bring us every entrée on your menu along with milk for me and whatever the lady wants to drink." He brushed his lips over her cheek. "What would you like?"

She turned her face into his and pressed her mouth to his ear. "For you to order something harder than milk. Keep up the pretense."

He knew what she meant but didn't like her thinking this had been nothing more than a game to him, rather than the most memorable evening he'd known. "What do you suggest?"

"Beer, at least. Alcoholic, but won't knock you on your ass. I'll have a liter of vodka."

He spoke to the server. "Two liters of vodka along with the other stuff I ordered."

"Right away." The server faced the crowd and clapped his hands. "Show's over. Please file out peacefully. The chariot races begin in fifteen."

The guys hooted and pumped their fists.

Rafael pressed his mouth to her ear. "Chariot races?"

"You don't want to know."

Maybe he would, though he didn't ask. Her squirms convinced him to stop leaning on her and to pull out.

Sprawled face up on the table, she rested her arm over her eyes. He sank to his knees and stroked her leg. "Sleepy?"

Despite his triple X-rated orgasm, he'd never been as alert.

She kept her eyes covered, face turned away. "Give me a sec and I'll be ready for the horse, then a cane, whip or whatever you want to use."

"Is that what you want to do? Is that what you want from me?"

She shrugged. "You're the Dom here. Your choice."

"Pretend I'm not your Master and that we're friends who can be straight with each other."

For once, she didn't have a smart retort—or any, for that matter.

He rested his hand on her thigh. "You're not able to do that for me?"

"No." Her voice trembled. "That's not how this works."

His gut clenched. After the fun they'd had and what they'd shared in here, he'd hoped she'd open up, not push him away again. "I don't care how this is supposed to play out. It's nothing more than a vacation from reality."

"It's who I am."

"Bull, you're more than this."

She rolled away. He stood and brought her back, his face above hers. "Look at me."

"No."

"Hon, I'm not asking, I'm telling you as your Dom."

"Now you want to role play?"

"Please?"

Sorrow brimmed in her eyes. What looked like a whole lot of love, too.

He stroked her bottom lip. "I'm not giving up on you and I'm not going to let you give up on me."

"You don't get the final vote."

"Maybe not, but I plan to swing you to my side."

She laughed softly. "I meant, your superiors won't let us happen."

"Do you want us to?"

Her mouth quivered.

She did. No lie detector could have gotten better results than the look on her face at this moment. "I'll figure something out. As long as I post regular reports and don't make any waves, they'll leave me alone. They'll never have to know about us."

"Until they notice you're not whizzing home any longer for your body cavity searches."

"I'll tell them I have too much work down here to even think about leaving."

"How long will they believe that?"

Forever, I hope. "I'll work it out."

"Great, but what if they want details? You're incapable of lying."

"I can learn."

"No." She gripped his arms. "I don't want you changing for me or becoming a lesser angel."

"Protecting you and us is the right thing to do. It's not a crime."

"Not yet, but it will be. What happens when I'm off parole? Even someone as rotten as I am can't be on it forever. They'll reassign you to someone else. Possibly to another universe. What then?"

"I'll have a plan for us to stay together. Everything will be all right."

"But —"

"Shh." He rested his finger on her lips. "We'll talk about this later." He inclined his head to the footfalls in the hall. "Sounds like our food's here."

She grabbed his wrist, bit his finger lightly then pulled it away. "Good. I could use some booze. Make that a lot. I want to get hammered."

"You need to stop worrying."

Chapter Eleven

Wynona had to hand it to Rafael. He was way more optimistic than her when it came to their uncertain future. He ate with abandon. She picked at her food with the enthusiasm of a death-row inmate faced with his last meal.

"You have to try these. Wow." He chomped on a rib slathered with barbecue sauce. The stuff coated his lips.

Their carnal play had mussed his hair. Dark locks spilled over his forehead and shoulders. Stubble dusted his upper lip, cheeks and chin. A woman with far more self-control than she had could still get lost in his eyes — their heavenly blue shade was spectacular. His strong features weren't simply sexy, they were kind too.

If he and she had been mortal and married, Wynona would have wished for a little boy with his looks and capacity for sweet grace.

She fingered sauce from his bottom lip and sucked the flavoring off her thumb. "When you were alive, did you ever hope for children of your own?"

He washed down the barbecue with a shot of vodka and shivered. "Gah, that sucks. How can you stand it?"

"Wait 'til the warmth hits."

He looked at her dumbly then breathed in and smiled. "Whoa. Like liquid sunshine rolling through you."

"Exactly."

He took another hit, grimaced then sighed. "When I was alive, I mainly focused on staying that way. Building a family wasn't in the picture. For a time, I considered my mistress might get pregnant because of our afternoon sessions. Never happened. Either she'd gone barren after having two kids or I was shooting blanks."

Wynona touched his hand. "Impossible. You're perfect."

He smiled self-consciously, his mouth orange from the sauce. "I want to believe I was merciful. Hard to do when people are treating you like crap and you're hungry most of the time, but there was this boy..." He shook his head.

"What?" She slipped her fingers beneath his chin and lifted his face so he had to look at her. "Tell me about him."

He pressed his lips to her palm and folded her hand in his. "He was lame, his left foot deformed. How he survived as long as he did in those days was a miracle. Most parents had enough trouble taking care of so-called normal kids. Flawed ones got dumped so they wouldn't be a burden. That's probably why he was alone all the time." Sadness filled his eyes. "He was a scrappy little guy, I'm guessing twelve, though he looked years younger, being so small and thin. He went through everyone's trash for stuff to eat. Annoyed the hell out of my master and mistress. They didn't like to see anything imperfect or dirty. Shook their worldview, I suppose. No matter how many times they had their guards smack the boy around to get him to leave, he came right back. Hunger does that to a person. My master decided to put poison on the food scraps to get rid of the kid for good. No muss, no fuss, no blood, just a body to dispose of."

She pressed her hand to her chest. "That's the most horrible thing I've heard in a long time, and I've heard plenty."

"Back then, some would have said my master was acting humanely. The boy had no future. In time, he would have starved anyway. I offered to hide the poisoned food in the trash."

"What? No." His casual admission shook Wynona to her core. "You couldn't have."

"I did. If I hadn't, someone else would have. I fed it to the vermin. When the boy showed up, as he always did, I warned him about the poison and gave him food I'd squirreled away from my meals. I told him where the untainted stuff would be in the future and not to touch anything except what I'd be leaving."

She hadn't believed she could have loved him more but she did. "You risked so much when you were hungry, too."

"I couldn't live with myself if I'd let him suffer."

"You saved his life." She threw her arms around him.

He hugged her tenderly. "I did what I could until I drowned."

She'd forgotten about that. "Only because you were trying to save the dog after you rescued your master's kids. My guess is they were probably snotty little fuckers like their father. You're a saint."

"Naw. I didn't volunteer to have lions tear me apart during the games because of my beliefs. Those were the brave souls, not me."

"Bull. You would have faced an entire army to save that kid and others."

"Maybe."

"Definitely. Don't argue with me."

His smile lit up his face. "I'd always rather make love."

Wynona wished she had known him from the moment she came into existence. "Do you think the boy survived?"

"Dunno. I've always liked to think he did, but I do tend to be a dreamer."

Tell me about it, especially concerning our situation. She pressed her face against his neck.

"Ah, folks?"

The server wearing the cock extender was back.

Wynona wanted to reap him for his interruption and might have if he hadn't already been dead. "Someone else wants to use the room?"

"In about ten, sorry, we're really swamped tonight. Before you take off, would you two care for a photo to commemorate your visit to the Double B?"

The picture might be all she'd have left of Rafael once his incurable optimism hit the unforgiving wall of their reality. She held his hand to her chest, wanting him more than she'd believed possible. "I'd like to. Do you mind?"

"It'll be fun."

Once the server had removed the phalluses from the saddle, she and Rafael posed on the horse together, each brandishing a liter of vodka and grinning for the camera. They laughed themselves breathless and kissed until she was weak.

He wrapped her in his cape and escorted her from the club, his arm around her protectively rather than possessively. Although being a submissive was nice, she had to admit this was better.

At the door, Yardley greeted them with a broad grin, taking in their sappy smiles and the booze they carried. "Do I have to ask if you two had a good time?"

Rafael hugged her. "It was the freaking best. Thanks. First thing tomorrow, I'm subscribing to your newsletter. Looking forward to info on your upcoming releases."

"If you could leave a review on my site for those you've seen, I'd be forever grateful."

"You bet. I'll tell my friends, too."

He couldn't have meant the ones in Heaven.

"Thanks." Yardley beamed. "Have a good one."

Wynona's glow lasted until she and Rafael reached the outside. Given that the club was truly in the middle of nowhere, they couldn't hop in a cab, plane or train to get back to her place. Walking was out of the question, too. His wings were the only option.

Maybe if she didn't look, she could keep the fantasy alive a little longer.

The swish of his unfurling wings was too much to resist, though she wished she had.

He rubbed her back. "It's all right."

Not even close. His feathers were solid black, possibly darker than hers. "You're screwed."

"Actually, I'm thrilled. A couple of times tonight, my back twitched really bad. I thought my feathers might have dissolved or fallen off, but they're good to go." He plucked at one. The thing didn't budge. "Same as always."

"They're supposed to be white. They may never be that way again."

"I don't care." He gathered her to him. "I'm not going to let anything ruin our evening. Next stop, our place."

She should have corrected him on that *our* but couldn't. From now until their hopes circled the drain, they were roomies. Wynona predicted their new arrangement would last five days tops, maybe six, before his superiors found out what he was doing and came down hard.

Back in her apartment, she uncapped the vodka. Rafael took the bottle from her and placed it and his on the counter, along with their pictures from the club. "We don't need booze to have fun."

She couldn't argue about that, but getting smashed would take the edge off her worry. "By fun do you mean vanilla, BDSM or the kind that tests your skill and restraint?"

Interest sparked in his gorgeous eyes. "You tell me."

"Ever play strip poker?"

"Not even the regular kind. I did see *The Cincinnati Kid* and *Rounders*, though."

"You're a real film buff, huh?"

"Never had much to do after work until I met you."

His answer was the best ever. Their non-future already bummed Wynona enough. She didn't want to also be jealous of his time with Ursula. "Want to play?"

"Sure. I assume that in strip poker we bet our clothes rather than chips."

"That's right."

"How's that going to work here? You're already naked except for your boots, stockings, nipple rings, collar and the bauble in your belly. I'm nearly there, too." He gestured to his well-ventilated tights.

"We can play reverse strip poker. Whoever loses has to put on a piece of clothing."

"Doesn't that defeat the purpose?"

"Not if you want to stay nude or nearly so. An incentive to win."

"Or lose. I don't mind covering up, but when it comes to you..." Mischief gleamed in his eyes. "I like the way you are now, so I don't mind losing to you at all."

"Okay, whoever wins has to put on a piece of clothing."

"Or throw the game."

He was too logical. "Fine. New rule. Whoever loses not only has to cover up but cedes an orgasm to the winner."

"Think you could manage losing a climax?"

"Think you could?"

"What kind of poker are we playing here, other than reverse strip? Texas Hold'em, 7-card stud, 5-card draw, Omaha?"

She frowned. "You said you've never played."

"Haven't. But I've had a lot of time to read up on the various games. Change your mind?" He leaned in. "Chicken?"

Wynona elbowed him away. "You choose. I'll beat your socks off."

"My tights will do. I want to be ready for all those orgasms you'll owe me."

She needed to wean Rafael from his bullheaded desire for her. Once she denied him sex for a few weeks, he might turn his sights to a good angel. Not Ursula, though. That would be too much to stomach. He'd have to choose another woman, unknown to Wynona, who would coax out his inherent decency, giving his wings a chance to revert to their original color.

Pollyanna had nothing on her.

The cards and oaths flew. Most of the obscenities came from him. He lost the first game and put on his cape. After his second loss, he ran out of his own clothes.

Wynona offered him her daintiest bra.

He grabbed a whip from her collection. "This matches my outfit."

"Play."

He lost the third game too and glared. "You're cheating."

"If that's what you want to call being skilled, go ahead. Hurt my feelings."

"I'll apologize as soon as I do that, which I haven't. I left my regular clothes at the service. Give me a sec to get them."

She gestured him back into the chair and again handed over her bra. "I'd rather you wear this."

"No."

"Chicken?"

He put it on his head and tied the straps under his chin like a bonnet. "Satisfied?"

She laughed.

He did too, scooped her from the chair and kissed her hard. When they came up for air, he pressed his cheek to hers. "Game's over."

He carried her to the bed.

As far as she was concerned, their play had only begun. Their boots clunked on the floor. She ripped off his tights. He did the same with her stockings and also removed her collar but left her body jewelry in place and pulled her down to the mattress.

She shot back up. "No vanilla, not yet. Stay where you are." She turned her back to him, straddled his lean hips and slid down until his sex was hers to feast on and hers was his for the taking.

They not only indulged, they wallowed in pleasure, bringing each other joy well into the afternoon.

* * * *

Rafael couldn't stop smiling. He didn't walk, he floated. If he lived past forever and a day, he'd never forget these moments or understand mortals' preoccupation with the great beyond or their desire for it. They already had so much on Earth from simply being alive. A chance to smell the morning air, see the sun rise, marvel at the endless bounty. Mostly, they had an opportunity to love, the greatest gift there was.

When time came for work, Wynona insisted they not arrive together in order to keep a low profile.

He nodded solemnly at her plan. "So that would be a lower profile than Zoe and her guys getting it on in a treatment room? Heather and MJ trying on fetish wear? Daemon and Heather making out behind the plants near her desk? Daemon talking about his cock and pretending he doesn't want to show it off when he does? Me hiding the hickeys you left on both my thighs and you covering up the one I put on your shoulder? Do I need to go on?"

She smacked his butt then pointed at him. "Stay here twenty minutes before you go in."

He stayed two, got dressed quickly and waited in a treatment room for her to arrive. Once she'd passed his door, he snuck out, wrapped his arm around her waist and swung her around.

She squealed excitedly.

He cut off the sound with his tongue and trapped her against the wall, his kiss white hot, his need for her immeasurable. Earthy growls and soft sighs spilled from her. She wrapped her leg around his and drove her fingers through his hair.

No way would he make it through tonight's endless shift without several long breaks. Maybe he should claim her evaluation was today and they needed to meet in her office, alone, with the lock thrown and a do-not-disturb sign on her door. Becca probably wouldn't buy his story, but he had to give it a shot.

With their mouths still joined, he eased Wynona from the wall and stumbled toward her office, kissing her hard, soft, anyway he could.

"Ah, Rafael?"

Becca. *Crud.* There went his plan to evaluate Wynona tonight. Tamping down his disappointment, he pulled his mouth from hers.

Wynona yanked him right back and shoved her tongue between his lips.

Loud throat clearing rang out. Deep and gritty, somewhat like Zoe's or a guy's. Stefin putting on a holier-than-thou show? Annoyed at the interruption, Rafael tore his mouth from Wynona's and was ready to give the intruder serious hell.

Frank, his supervisor, stood next to Becca. Her features were tight with dismay. Frank looked ready to crumble from old age or what he'd just seen, his wrinkles deeper, noggin even balder, his frail form swallowed by his baby-blue jogging suit.

Rafael opened his mouth to explain, lie and plead. "Ah..."

Wynona gave him an odd look, glanced at Frank and turned paler than she usually was. "Oh, my God, you're him. Boss man."

Becca took Wynona's arm. "Rafael and his supervisor need to talk. You and I can go to my office."

"No." She pulled her arm away and fisted her fingers in Frank's top. "You and I need to have a word."

Rafael didn't know what in the hell she was doing but didn't think her behavior would help matters. He pried her fingers off Frank. "Go with Becca."

"No." She got in Frank's face. He stepped back. She followed. "You have the wrong idea about this."

"I wish it were so."

"It is, dammit."

He cowered. "Are you going to beat me up?"

"Not if you take off. Go." She pointed at the ceiling.

"I can't leave and forget this. If you give me a second, I'll explain why."

"You have three. One, two—"

He whipped a smartphone from his pocket and turned the screen to her.

Rafael hurried over to look and wished he hadn't. Someone from last night had ignored the warning about no recordings. The Double B looked more spacious than the room actually was, his cock a real whopper, his orgasmic grimace exactly as he'd imagined. Surprisingly, his costume didn't look as dumb as he'd thought. Wynona, of course, was exquisite.

"You're not listening." She smacked the phone from Frank's hand. It hit the wall and clattered on the floor. "Everything's my fault. I conned him."

Rafael frowned. "The fuck you did."

"Please." Frank held his hand to his throat. "Isn't the video bad enough? Now you're talking like a demon?"

He wasn't ashamed. Stefin, Anatol, Taro and Zoe had gutter mouths but they were good people. As far as the video was concerned, it was pure awesome, no matter what anyone said. He spoke to Wynona. "You're gorgeous."

She focused on Frank. "That's magic talking, including the wish, potion and spell I used on him. Just in case that stuff didn't take, I poisoned his food and drink so he wouldn't give me a hard time. No way was I going through that again with another PO after that prick Xavier. Rafael had nothing to do with this. I take full responsibility." She thrust out her hands, wrists together. "Slap on the cuffs and take me to Hell. I deserve the shittiest dungeon in solitary."

Rafael kissed her knuckles.

She whimpered and pushed him away then shoved her fists at Frank. "Go on. I'm the bad guy. He's innocent."

Rafael eased her aside. "What happened was my idea. I came on to her. She refused me repeatedly, so I pulled rank as her PO, telling her she had to sleep with me or else."

"Ah, that's sexual harassment." Becca shook her head. "A definite no-no."

Wynona sneered. "When he said that to me, it was only a joke. He's perfect."

Rafael resisted a sigh. If anything, he'd become more like a flawed human down here and that was okay. Caring about another person was what counted. "I'm not perfect."

He unfurled his wings.

Several gasps filled the hall. Zoe, her guys, Constance, Heather, Daemon and MJ stared at Rafael's black feathers.

Wynona smacked his arm. "What is the matter with you?"

"Nothing. I love you." He looked down his nose at Frank. "That's not a crime."

"Actually, it is for a good angel to fall in love with a reaper. Simply not done."

He shrugged. "No prob. I refuse to be a good angel any longer. I want to be a reaper now."

"No!" Wynona punched Frank's biceps. "Talk some sense into him."

Rafael crossed his arms. "Won't do any good. I want to stay down here and reap with you."

"Are you trying to kill me? Do you have any idea how awful the job is? The anguish of taking someone whose time shouldn't have come, like kids, parents and good people? Having everyone scorn and loathe you?"

"We can comfort each other." He uncrossed his arms and embraced her.

She sagged against him then stiffened and pulled away. "Becca, cast a spell on him so he changes his mind."

Rafael pressed his mouth to her ear. "Sure you want that, given her lousy spells? No telling what I'll end up doing or being. She might turn me into a woman."

"MJ." Wynona pointed at her. "Grant my wish, please. I want his feathers white again so he can go back to Heaven."

"Where I don't want to be." He frowned at MJ. "If you grant any of Wynona's wishes without my written consent, I'll sue."

MJ lifted her shoulders. "If he doesn't want this, my hands are tied. Same with Heather healing him. No use asking her."

Wynona bared her teeth at Frank. "You're his supervisor. You could intervene and okay the wish, potion, spell, healing, whatever."

"That's not what I had in mind."

"You can't let him rot in Hell." She punched Frank's other biceps. "What kind of a good angel are you?"

"A bruised one." He skittered back and rubbed his arm. "Is there a private place where the three of us can talk without violence?"

"No." Wynona stood between him and Rafael. "If you lift one finger to take him anywhere but Heaven, I want witnesses. I'll turn you in. I'll sic the Horsemen of the Apocalypse and the hounds of Hell on you."

"Guess we'll talk out here, then."

Becca and the others edged closer.

Frank looked as if he'd aged several centuries. He spoke to Rafael. "You really want her, huh?"

"She's my only reason for being."

Wynona bounced on her heels. "Quit saying that."

"Okay, here's the thing." Frank folded his hands. "After I saw the recording, I conferred with my superiors. They suggested several solutions, but none seemed right. Then I had a thought."

Wynona frowned. "What kind?"

He focused on Rafael. "I know you well enough to see how much you love her. I kept waiting for you to look at Ursula that way, but I'm a realist. As they say, ain't gonna happen. If you want to become a reaper, that's your choice. I can grant the change in status and position."

Rafael pumped his fist.

Wynona moaned. "That's no freaking solution. What is the matter with you?"

"Hear me out." Frank cleared his throat. "After witnessing your meltdown, I can see how much you love Rafael. Therefore, I can grant you a change from reaper to good angel so you can be with him and you can both serve Heaven. Your choice."

Rafael's mouth fell open.

For once, Wynona was speechless.

Becca rushed to them. "Choose good angel, please."

Zoe and the others concurred.

"Hold it." Wynona held up her hand. "Is this a trick? How can I suddenly be a good angel? I've been on stinking parole for eons. You guys keep threatening me with the slammer."

"Our mistake." Frank gave her a sheepish smile. "Rafael's reports opened our eyes to who you really are. You've fought to keep from reaping innocent children and people with pure hearts. You wanted Death to target the greedy and cruel to make the world a better place. You never had a choice in what you were. You've earned your white wings and a soul...if you want them."

Rafael couldn't believe such a miracle had happened. He cupped her face. "Please say you do."

"Fucking A." She threw her arms around him.

The staff cheered.

This time, Frank's smile reached his eyes. "I have full faith you two will make one helluva team."

Epilogue

Several months later

Although Valentine's Day wasn't a huge deal for supernaturals like Halloween, the lovers' holiday did get its due at the service.

Sumptuous floral arrangements with colorful balloons decorated Heather's desk, courtesy of Daemon and MJ. Heather, in turn, had given him a candy tree made of Milky Ways, Snickers, Reese's Peanut Butter Cups, Hershey's and Butterfinger candy bars. MJ proudly wore her gift from Heather, a scarlet body stocking embroidered in all the right places to make it nominally decent but still as racy as anything found at Frederick's of Hollywood.

Taro, Anatol and Stefin had decorated Zoe's office with carrion flowers, her fave. The pretty but nasty-smelling blossoms were in onyx vases with large black bows embossed with hearts. She'd surprised them with eternity passes to every club in the second circle of Hell.

Also known as Lust. Now, when they took her there, figuratively and literally, they didn't have to shell out the bucks.

Becca and Constance had really hauled in the loot, getting candy, flowers and jewelry from their guys. Becca wore her gorgeous Goth necklace made of satin, lace, black pearls and marcasite hearts. She also flashed an enormous diamond ring Eric had given her at breakfast. Gabe had done the same for Constance, surprising her with an engagement ring in between bites of ham and eggs. It looked like the service would soon be hosting two bachelorette parties.

Wynona couldn't have been happier for them or her and Rafael. They'd spent the morning and afternoon in each other's arms, exchanging the best gifts the world offered…their promise to always love and respect each other, to share their worries and to celebrate each day. They'd also booked the Double B for tonight to raise some serious hell.

Even good angels had to have fun. Especially after working so hard.

During these last months, she'd hit the books, studying for her white feathers and soul. Last week, she'd graduated the program and gotten them. Rafael's wings had returned to their natural color the moment she'd agreed to cross over to his side. No matter how randy they got, their feathers remained pristine. What happened between them sexually wasn't what counted, only how they treated others.

Rafael, as always, was perfect. He'd left his job as a parole officer to be a guardian angel to troubled kids. He and Wynona would never have their own children, but they could guide those in need.

She was doing her part at the service, counseling clients on how to behave in mortal relationships, teaching them to honor their lovers rather than using supernatural powers to con them, and to respect boundaries, too. The zombies had the most trouble setting limits. They kept coming and coming and coming. Wynona hung in there, determined to whip them and the other supernaturals into shape.

Given that tonight was for lovers, she had a ton of appointments, but she needed time with her man first.

With her office door locked, she luxuriated in Rafael's strength and heat, savoring these last moments they'd have before he took off. Tonight, he'd watch over a teen on the verge of joining a gang. The poor kid was short and puny and needed the bangers for his own protection more than anything else. She had no doubt Rafael would turn the boy around, giving him a chance at a real future.

With love, anything was possible.

She finally eased her mouth from his and swatted his butt. "You gotta go. Me, too. We'll meet here after we're both through with business."

His Dom costume was in her bottom desk drawer. She'd already dressed for fun in a red leather sheath that dipped low in front and back with strategically placed laces to keep her respectable. Her temporary heart tats and silver stilettos were positively sinful.

Being a good angel didn't mean looking like a nun.

With her arm through his, she ushered Rafael to the hall so he could say bye to everyone before soaring through the ceiling.

He stopped short of the reception area.

Heather was speaking to a pretty young woman in a frumpy tan suit. The skirt fell to mid-calf. The jacket was equally boxy and hid any curves she might have. She'd buttoned her ecru blouse to her throat, had on sensible cream shoes that were way past ugly and had pulled her light brown hair into a bun so tight her eyebrows arched.

Poor thing needed to loosen up, wear brighter colors and get lost. She was either a mortal who'd stumbled unwittingly into this place, was here to talk salvation on behalf of a ministry or had arrived for the unlikeliest scenario of all. She actually did belong here.

Wynona pressed against Rafael. "Think she's from SACS and is checking this place out to stash a rebel reaper here?"

"Nope. She's Ursula."

"Ah…oh."

Ursula had spotted them. She rushed their way waving her hand. "Hey, Rafael."

"Hey there. Gotta go." He pecked Wynona's cheek and ascended like a rocket.

Wynona would have followed but didn't want Ursula to feel worse than she already did. She slumped, dragging her padded shoulders with her. Wynona cleared her throat. "Hi. I'm—"

"I know who you are. Everyone in Heaven does. We've had meetings about you and Rafael. How your love conquered all."

Aw, that's so sweet.

Ursula whimpered. "He didn't have to run away from me. I know he worships you." She gestured to Wynona's scandalous outfit. "What man wouldn't?"

She recalled the dark times when everyone had detested her and she'd hurt as badly as Ursula did now. "Rafael didn't mean to cut out so abruptly. He had to leave for an important case. Actually, he often speaks of you."

"Oh, yeah? Is it good?"

More like bland and disinterested. "He said you're great at your job."

She waved away the compliment. "Anyone can file stuff. Once St. Peter finally okayed the computers, there wasn't much work for admin staff to do. You have to help me."

Not if she wanted Rafael back. "Sorry, I'm not following."

"I want a makeover to be like you." She pulled back her shoulders. "I want some super-duper action from a young man who's not afraid to be bold."

Snagging that bad boy would be easier if Ursula got hip with her language and clothes. "Does your supervisor know you're here?"

Ursula lifted her chin. "I'm on vacation. I have fifty years saved up from never taking a day off. Change me. Release my inner beast. Make me like you. I have the time."

Wynona wanted to run until she recalled how screwed up she'd been when Rafael had first come there. He'd given her a chance to choose love and stuck with her until she'd become the woman she was always meant to be.

"Let's talk in my office." She slipped her arm around Ursula's shoulders and guided her into the room.

It was going to be a long night, but hey, this was the right thing to do.

Something Rafael would have agreed on, despite his hasty exit. Tonight, when they were alone and in each other's arms, she'd tell him how good she'd been at work and how bad she intended to be in their bed. He'd brag on her, of course, saying she was the most wonderful being he'd ever known. Then he'd show her what paradise really was—a man and a woman's everlasting love that even Heaven couldn't compete with.

Want to see more from this author? Here's a taster for you to enjoy!

Taming the Beast: Seducing the Beast
Tina Donahue

Excerpt

Ursula sagged in her chair, hand over her eyes. For three weeks she'd gone through treatment at From Crud to Stud, a New Orleans makeover service for supernatural beings. Instead of these sessions turning her into a bad girl who drew hot men to her, she was still the same blah, frumpy good angel she'd been since ancient times. Talk about her decency getting old and the shameless indulgence she craved not happening as easily as she'd hoped.

She seemed doomed to spend her life alone and unwanted. Her mouth trembled. "This isn't working. It's never going to, for me, is it?"

Wynona kept her peace.

No surprise. Since Wynona had converted from a reaper to a good angel, she couldn't skirt the truth any longer, not even to spare a client's feelings. However, her eyes would reveal the sorry state of things.

Steeled for the worst, Ursula peeked through her fingers.

Wynona grinned at her smartphone screen. Her thumbs flew over the keyboard.

Ursula gritted her teeth. "Tell Rafael I said hi." After all, she and he had been going together when he'd dumped her for Wynona.

Her gaze inched up, pale cheeks flushing. Not from embarrassment...arousal. Her glazed eyes were a dead giveaway. She killed her goofy look, texted fast then put her phone, screen side down, on the treatment table. Brutal leather restraints hung from the arm and leg rests. Someone, or something, slammed into the wall behind them, followed by an unholy hiss.

Wynona arched her slender eyebrows. "How's it going?"

Scratching noises flowed from the room on the other side. Sounded like a were trying to claw through the wall to escape the ghastly treatment awaiting him. Ursula understood his pain. "You tell me. I still don't look, act or think like you."

Wynona was perfect in the looks department and blithely uninhibited around men, especially Rafael. Although tall and slender, she had enviable curves, like a Victoria's Secret model, her ample bosom not drooping as Ursula's did, her long legs fueling men's sinful dreams. Tonight, she wore a leather outfit, as usual, this one a deep rust shade. The long-sleeved top stopped beneath her breasts to reveal a creamy expanse of her torso. The band on her snug skirt grazed her navel. Her waist-length hair was white, her eyes silvery, her features exquisite.

Ursula hung her head. "I'd settle for being a millionth of what you are. You don't even get the frizzies when the weather's bad."

Rain drummed the roof and windows. The air was soupier than normal in the French Quarter and kinked Ursula's hair.

Wynona flicked her hand dismissively. Her lavender fragrance, sweet yet sultry, wafted close. "No way am I special. The way I look has zero to do with magic. Like other women, particularly mortals, I use industrial-strength conditioner available at any Walgreens. By the way, don't waste your dough on generic junk. Pantene kicks serious ass."

"If I rub it all over me, will I be like you?" *Sexy and confident, able to use bad words, indulge in indecent thoughts and get a hot guy?*

"You want to be the best of who you are, sweetie. No one else." Wynona squeezed Ursula's knee. "That's why we're using the latest technology to help you reach your goal." She'd hooked her up to an aversion therapy machine. Whenever a drab or boring woman popped up on the computer screen, the device zapped Ursula to teach her that stuff was blah. Thus far, they'd gone through most of Dr. Amy Farrah Fowler's scenes in *The Big Bang Theory*.

Despite the electricity frying her brain cells, she still found Amy's modest skirts, plaid blouses, oversized sweaters and sensible shoes rather attractive. "I don't think this is working."

Wynona played with the dial. "Maybe it's time to increase the voltage."

"If I were human, you would have electrocuted me long ago."

"No pain, no gain, right?"

"What pain? I'm beginning to like the jolts." Flushing, she squeezed her thighs together and gestured to her lady parts between them. "Down there."

"Yeah?" Wynona regarded the device with new interest. "Better than a motorized dildo, huh?"

There was no comparison. Amazon promised to deliver her machine before Friday, along with a beige sweater similar to Amy's in the latest episode. Ursula fantasized about wearing nothing except the cashmere and blubbering in ecstasy from each savage shock. Unfortunately, that didn't solve her problem.

"I don't think this is going to work." She pulled off the electrodes stuck to her temples, neck and wrists. "Let's cut through this other stuff and go for magic. A potion or spell to make me like you. Several if that's what I need."

"I'm flattered, but, no. The only way your makeover will succeed is for you to do the work, beginning with an attitude adjustment."

The were in the next room howled then panted loudly. "No, no, no," he shrieked. "I don't wanna!"

"Too bad," the staffer growled. "Get on the damn table."

"No. I—"

His scream cut off his protest. Other rooms pulsed with client moans and wails. Enforcers ran down the hall, shouting oaths and ordering customers to behave.

Ursula grabbed Wynona's soft, delicate hands. Even her knuckles were amazing. "Why can't we take a shortcut with this? Are you afraid that when I'm like you, I'll try to take Rafael away?"

Wynona turned her wrists and dug her nails into Ursula's palms. "Were you planning on doing that?"

Not any longer. She bit back a wince at the pain. "No."

Wynona released her. "You do realize potions and spells come with their own problems, right? It's like modern medicine. Ever see commercials for the newest wonder drugs? They'll cure insomnia, depression, rashes, shitty personalities, whatever, but they may also make you go blind, shrivel your lungs, stop your heart or keep you from swallowing for the rest of your life, which makes your initial complaint seem pretty tame in comparison."

"Shouldn't magic be more precise by calling on the dark powers?"

"What dark powers? All we have is Becca." Wynona scooted her chair closer and leaned in. "When Daemon wanted to ditch his satyr legs and hooves to look totally human, Becca forgot to give him feet until Heather had a meltdown."

Ursula pressed her hand to her chest. Heather was a good fairy and healer who worked as the receptionist here. Daemon, her boyfriend, was on the enforcement team. "Does Becca usually forget stuff like that?"

"Let's just say she's not the best witch on planet Earth. Before she and Eric got together, she gave him a potion that made him bald, rather than releasing his inner beast to turn him into a bad boy. Poor guy thought he was too nice, which made him lose the babes."

"He wanted other women, not her, so she made him bald?"

"What? No! Since she's lousy at spells and potions, she asked for her mom's help. Rowena's first-rate but warned magic could have unknown effects, especially on a minor god like him. Thankfully, everything worked out, but you don't want to go through that." She patted Ursula's shoulder. "A guy should love you for who you are, not who you think you want to be."

Easy for her to say. Rafael had been Wynona's parole officer when she'd been a rebel reaper, snatching souls before their time. Rather than keeping her on the straight and narrow, he'd begged her to corrupt him and had been willing to give up Heaven, his white wings and future for her. Nothing mattered, except having her love.

Ursula ached with envy. Paradise was nice but nothing without a guy to share the good stuff with. "You didn't have to change for Rafael because you're perfect. I'm not. No one's going to like me as I am."

"You're wrong. Rafael wanted me despite my faults." She shrugged. "We just clicked."

"You knew right away you were right for each other?"

"We both fought it, but yeah. You know when it fits."

She figured clicking and knowing weren't in her future since men never noticed her. If she wanted even a zillionth of what Wynona had, she'd have to be bold. "I'd like to try magic. I don't want to waste another minute."

"You haven't been at this that long." She fiddled with the machine and zapped herself lightly. A throaty hum poured from her followed by a breathless sigh and goofy grin. "Give it a chance. You have vacation time saved up."

Fifty years to be precise, since she'd never taken an hour off from her admin job in Heaven. She stood. "No. I'm going to talk to Becca."

Wynona tapped her foot, a sure sign she was frustrated, but she inhaled deeply and calmed. "I'll have a word with her. Go on, sit. I'll be back as soon as I can."

She reached the door, pivoted and returned for her smartphone. Too bad. Ursula had wanted to read Rafael's comments. She suspected they were filled with fire and passion. Perhaps a few naughty words, too. Nothing like his former bland relationship with her. Their dates and bed-play had been more well-mannered than a senior citizens' mixer.

She'd always believed he'd been that way with her because he was an honorable man. After all, he'd earned his wings by keeping two children from drowning during Roman times and had lost his own life in the rescue. To save their pet dog, no less. What other guy would have done so for an animal that wasn't even his? Although he was better looking than the male models on romance novel covers, his allure had never made him pushy or bold during their time together. They'd kissed without exchanging tongues, made love missionary-style with the lights off and always kept most of their clothes on.

Their physical encounters were all she knew about sex. As far as their mild emotional connection went, she'd thought that was the way things should be between a woman and a man.

Then he'd met Wynona, released his beast and threatened to leave Heaven if he couldn't have her carnally and tenderly, making their souls one for eternity.

That put the kibosh on his and Ursula's limp courtship. Even if he'd still wanted her, his so-so passion wasn't enough any longer. She hungered for a man who'd turn her inside out and who would afford her unleashed desire, at least for a little while.

In preparation for her change from drab to dynamite, she googled women's leather outfits. The skirts looked too tight and the tops downright uncomfortable. However, if this was the price for a good time, so be it. She filled her Amazon cart.

"Hey, how you doin'?" The male voice rumbled like quiet thunder past the closed door.

Something inside her fluttered. She lifted her face.

In the hall, scuffles broke out. Something slammed against the door and other places, rattling the framed business license hanging above the desk.

A woman moaned.

The same male voice grunted lewdly.

"Hey!" Daemon's shout didn't stop the lusty noises. The sounds traveled to the right and grew fainter.

Footfalls bounded past.

Ursula hurried into the hall. At the far end, Heather was pressed against a door, her arms flailing. A tall man snuggled into her and sucked her throat. Given her rounded eyes and bared teeth, she wasn't loving it.

"Dammit, get away from her." Daemon grabbed the guy's arm. "She belongs to me."

Ursula had never heard a more romantic declaration.

The other man flicked Daemon off like a pesky gnat, which sent him flying backward. He bounced off the wall and dropped to the floor face down, his black shirt and pants askew.

Heather yelped. "You hurt him. How could you?" She kneed the guy.

He gasped and cradled his injured groin.

Her complexion went even paler. "I'm so sorry." She bounced on her heels and flapped her hands. "I shouldn't have done that. I'm so sorry."

Daemon groaned.

She shoved the guy away and darted past, white blouse and skirt bobbing. Her baby powder scent filled the space. Upon reaching Daemon's side, she dropped to her knees.

Heat radiated from the other man, as welcome on this cool, clammy night as hot chocolate was during a snowstorm.

Unable to help herself, Ursula edged closer.

His hair was thick and wavy. The dark brown locks tumbled over his forehead and curled around his ears. Classical Greek features made him movie-star handsome. Dark stubble dusted his firm jaw, upper lip and cheeks.

Warmth flooded her.

She had an insane urge to cup his beautiful face and stroke his bronze skin. Both were impossibly virile, the same as his broad shoulders and muscular arms. A black tee hugged his firm pecs, ripped abs and bruising biceps. He had a tribal tattoo on the right one that mesmerized her. Her nipples tightened.

His low-slung jeans left nothing to the imagination. He stopped cupping himself and revealed the enormous bulge behind his fly.

Her mouth got even drier.

"Tell me where Farron hurt you." Heather touched Daemon as a blind woman would, lingering on every spot, especially the X-rated ones. Color flooded her cheeks. Desire welled in her eyes. "I'll make it better."

The guy, Farron, snorted and made a beeline for them.

Ursula blocked him.

He reared back. Surprise crossed his features at her presence and interference. Confusion replaced it.

What could she say? She had no idea why she'd stopped him except it seemed the right thing to do. Not for Heather or Daemon, for her.

She pushed to her toes and craned her neck to drink in his straight nose, slightly flared nostrils and full mouth. Far too often, she'd dreamed of lips like his, despite the danger carnal thoughts posed to a good angel. Although her soul was pure, she was also a woman and indulged in his animal magnetism. In human years, he was probably thirty or so. Supernaturally, he was a demon and had likely been around since time began. Tiny flames flickered in his black eyes. His scent was of the Earth and its deepest depths. The sulfur smell alone should have warned her off. Instead, his fragrance drew her to him, the same as his heat.

A zombie groaned in the room behind him.

He didn't bother looking over, regarding her instead. He frowned. "What?"

If she could have formed words, she would have introduced herself. Unfortunately, she didn't have enough strength left to smile. Drooling was her sole option.

"What the hell?" Stefin, a beefy Russian with blond hair, rushed down the hall, followed by redheaded Taro then Anatol, who sported long dreadlocks as dark as his complexion. All three were demons and enforcers there who kept clients from getting too frisky. They, like Daemon, wore black shirts and pants.

Farron grinned at the trio. His smile carved deep dimples in both cheeks, making him even more adorable.

Her legs wavered.

"Loosen up." He gave the guys a careless shrug. "I was only having a little fun."

"Not with Heather, you don't." Daemon slung his arm around her and planted his hand smack on her breast.

She turned bright pink but sagged against him.

Farron gestured in surrender. "Fine with me. Which room is mine?" He pivoted away and almost fell over Ursula.

She lifted her face to his.

He stepped back.

Stefin joined him. "I'm in charge here." He slammed his fist into his chest, his muscles thick like his accent. Taro and Anatol rolled their eyes. Stefin glared at Farron. "You'll go to the room I tell you to go to."

"Is that so?" Farron lifted his hand.

Stefin and the other demons did the same.

Power from the dark side zoomed between them.

Ursula skittered out of harm's way.

Lights flickered. Air sizzled. Farron held his own against the guys, the battle a Mexican standoff.

He laughed. A booming sound filled with mischief and surprising joy.

Enthralled, Ursula staggered toward him.

He looked over.

Taro hurled a new blast, a mega flash that turned everything blinding white. Once colors bled back in, an invisible force pinned Farron's arms to his sides. His large feet dangled several inches above the floor.

"In there." Stefin gulped air and inclined his head to the left. Together, he and the guys used their powers to push Farron into the room, his back to it.

She followed.

He stared at her, eyes widened. "*What*?"

Before she could manage a word, Anatol slammed the door and locked it. She could have walked through the barrier, an easy thing for a good angel, but that would have been rude. Disappointed, she slouched against the wall.

"Ah, guys, get a room, all right?" Wynona shook her head at Heather and Daemon making out on the floor more passionately than most couples did in bed. She stepped around them and strode to Ursula. "What are you doing out here?"

She opened her mouth but still couldn't speak.

Wynona eyed her. "Are you okay?"

Uncertain, Ursula turned to Farron's room. It was eerily quiet, considering four uncivilized males lurked inside.

"What happened to your hair?"

At Wynona's question, Ursula patted her bun, surprised to find it twice its normal size. The rest of her slicked-back do was also frizzed and poofy.

"I'll write down the name of the Pantene conditioner I use and give you an online coupon I found. Come on." Wynona steered her back into the treatment room and shut the door. "Okay, I talked to Becca. And she—"

"Who is he?"

"—agrees with me. Wait. What? Who is who?"

"The guy Anatol, Taro and Stefin hauled into the treatment room." She jabbed her thumb in that direction. "His name's Farron. Who is he? What's his story?"

"Why?"

Heat poured through Ursula. Her face burned as it never had during her time on Earth and in Heaven. "I want him."

He is the one. We fit.

Rarely had Farron been as unsettled, which surprised him.

After his literal fall from grace, he'd spent eons in Hell with nothing fazing him. Not the brimstone, heat or Satan's constant bitching about how the Big Guy, aka God, refused to see another point of view and had booted S out, leaving him nowhere to go except Hell where even the most fervent masochist would feel put upon. Yeah, yeah, yeah. Farron had heard it all, nodded agreeably and made the best of things, which included having wicked fun twenty-four-seven. Messing with people's heads was a delight. Screwing with women... Fuck, there wasn't much to compete with that. Except a new challenge. Something to make his balls and cock sing.

He couldn't tear his attention from the hall. Given the sounds, Heather and Daemon were going at each other like wild animals, their cooing punctuated by indecent moans and grunts.

Farron had hoped she'd taste sweeter than she had, being a good fairy and all. Oddly enough, her innocence hadn't stirred him as he'd expected. What a bummer. He'd come here to tame his beast so he could meet virtuous babes, mortal or otherwise, for a change of pace. In Hell, there were no shrinking violets. If those ladies wanted a ride, they'd jump him without pause, apology or regret. He did the same with them. After an eternity filled with excess, getting it on with someone reserved sounded rather exciting.

Not Heather, though. She'd been so cool within his embrace he'd had trouble keeping warm. A first since his banishment. Her kneeing his nuts hadn't stoked his lust, either. His boys still ached, yet his rod stood at full-attention and tilted toward the hall.

Taro finished restraining Farron with the leather straps on the treatment table, after which Anatol added a powerful force field.

Stefin rocked on his heels. "Dare to make a move and we'll leave you here forever."

"Yeah?" Farron broke through the left restraint and scratched his nose.

Growling, Stefin wrestled Farron's arm down and held it while the others secured the strap. Farron twisted his right wrist, eager to pop loose from that restraint.

"I don't think so." Despite his lilting French accent and mild manner, Anatol held his fist over Farron's groin. "Stay put or I'll crack your nuts. None of us will let Heather fix them, either."

As a healer, she mended customers' physical problems at the service.

Taro chuckled. "I doubt she'd want to touch that part of him."

He had a point. She hadn't liked his tongue skimming her lips, wanting inside her mouth. For a few seconds, he'd worried she'd unclench her teeth and bite the tip off. The same reaction he'd gotten from mortal babes when he'd gotten too playful. Their response he was beginning to understand. However, what else had happened in the hall bewildered him. "Who is she?"

Stefin scratched his underarm. "A good fairy. Isn't that obvious with her white clothes, blonde hair, pale complexion and constant apologies?"

"Not Heather. The chick who was in the hall with us."

Stefin made a face. "What chick? You mean like baby poultry?" He bumped Anatol's arm. "Is Constance having one of her voodoo ceremonies tonight?"

"I think he means a woman, not a chicken."

"Ding, ding, ding." Farron smiled at Anatol. "You win the prize. So who is she?"

"I didn't see anyone." He glanced at Taro. "You?"

"Not me. You?"

Stefin shook his head.

Holy fuck, she'd been there, big as life, staring, putting him off his game and allowing the three stooges to get the upper-hand. "I almost fell over her. She's about five-five, light brown hair pulled back, no makeup, and wore a tan business suit with a white, high-necked blouse, long skirt and yukky shoes like nurses or old ladies prefer. I can't say for sure—given all she had on—but she seems to have a great rack, nice flare to her hips too. Smells clean, kind of soapy, you know? Her eyes are hazel, more on the golden side than brown. She has long, dark lashes, a creamy complexion with a touch of pink in her cheeks and her face is on the sweet-pretty side, rather than beautiful. If I had to guess, I'd say she's early to mid-twenties in human years."

The guys traded glances.

Farron wasn't surprised. He hadn't realized he'd noticed so much about her. His uneasiness returned, worrying him that kissing Heather had screwed with his brain, putting chaste desires there rather than his usual X-rated ones. The woman he'd seen certainly wasn't a *Hustler* centerfold. "You guys honestly didn't notice another female out there dressed like a missionary or one of the Duggars?"

Stefin grabbed a clipboard. "The last time I saw anyone who looked like that was when Ursula came in for her appointment."

Ech, what a name. Sounded like a parochial school teacher. "She's a nun? A demon possessed her and the service is trying to draw the evil one out?"

Maybe that's why she'd stared. She still felt the treatment effects.

Taro leaned against the counter. "Ursula was Rafael's main squeeze until he met Wynona, who used to be a reaper, but now she's a good angel like him, but only after she tried to put him off with Olaf, who's a reaper, too."

"Wait." Anatol put up his hand. "Rafael thought she was using Olaf to make him jealous after he pissed her off by kissing her and saying Becca told him to do so."

"I haven't a clue how Olaf fits into this." Taro spoke to Farron. "As far as getting Rafael to leave her be, so he wouldn't corrupt himself, Wynona asked Becca to mix a potion to turn his black wings white again. She wouldn't without his consent. I reckon we're all grateful for that, since her piss-poor potion probably would have given him another head. Constance wouldn't help, either, said it was against industry standards for her to remove his memories of Wynona without him knowing about it. No dice with MJ, too, who insisted on a contract signed in triplicate before she granted any wishes. Heather, being Heather, was too afraid to do anything she considered wrong, including healing his fucked-up wings, which pretty much left Wynona with no choice except to get down and dirty with Rafael until Frank found out and paid a visit to put a stop to that shit, which, oddly enough, had Wynona getting white wings instead of her black ones."

This was worse than trying to follow a plot on *Nashville*. Taro's country-western accent was as bad as the characters' twangs on the show. "And that makes Ursula…"

"Screwed." Stefin pointed his pen. "Though not literally."

"Yeah, I get that. Was Rafael once her guardian angel? She's mortal and he saved her life or soul or something and they got together then?"

They laughed.

Stefin wrote on his clipboard. "She's a good angel, like Rafael. Actually, better than him, never doing anything wrong, no bad thoughts, no fun, dull as dirt, totally forgettable."

Farron got that, too, since they hadn't noticed Ursula. He had, big-time, and so had his cock. The dumb thing twitched and pointed at the hall, where he'd last seen her.

Home of Erotic Romance

Sign up for our newsletter and find out about all our romance book releases, eBook sales and promotions, sneak peeks and FREE romance books!

About the Author

Tina is an Amazon and international bestselling novelist who writes passionate romance for every taste—'heat with heart'—for traditional publishers and indie. Booklist, Publisher's Weekly, Romantic Times and numerous online sites have praised her work. She's won Readers' Choice Awards, was named a finalist in the EPIC competition, received a Book of the Year award, The Golden Nib Award, awards of merit in the RWA Holt Medallion competitions, and second place in the NEC RWA contests. She's featured in the Novel & Short Story Writer's Market. Before penning romances, she worked at a major Hollywood production company in Story Direction.

Tina loves to hear from readers. You can find her contact information, website details and author profile page at https://www.totallybound.com